RAPTURE AND THE SECOND COMING

RAPTURE
AND
THE SECOND COMING

by

Wendy Borgstrom

Boston: Alyson Publications, Inc.

Published as a trade paperback original by
Alyson Publications, Inc., 40 Plympton St., Boston, MA 02118.
Distributed in the U.K. by
GMP Publishers, P.O. Box 247, London, N17 9QR, England.

First edition, first printing, May 1990.

Library of Congress catalog card number 90-583

ISBN 1-55583-166-4

5 4 3 2

To Nickie,
whose contempt for real literature
inspired this work.

And to Mark,
the Angel who hovered.

Perfect submission, perfect delight,
visions of rapture burst on my sight.

&INTRODUCTION

I lay in my bed and stared up at the ceiling in the dark. Inside, I was boiling. My gut churned with a mixture of excitement and despair.

She lay in the other bed. She was wearing those soft, silky pajamas. Her covers were off, and in the moonlight, I could see her — if I dared to look — lying on her back. Her chest was rising up and down, barely discernible, as she took gentle breaths.

She was so close. Our beds were separated only by a small table. It was three feet — an arm's length away — and yet, it might as well have been a mile.

It had been more than two months since I first approached her with my feelings, naked and raw. I ached for her and I had to let her know it. I needed to know if there was any chance for us.

She took a lot of time answering me that night. She didn't want me to think that she didn't feel something too. Maybe as strongly as I did. But she wasn't able to let go — to consummate those feelings. Making love with a woman scared her, thoroughly. She felt it was wrong.

Now I lay there, still aching for her. If anything, my desire for her had increased over the weeks. I would explode if things continued on as they did. It was time to talk again. I wondered if she was awake.

I looked over at her, carefully. I thought I saw her eyes open and close. She was awake. My eyes returned to study that spot on the ceiling. I opened my mouth and hoped that words would form and come out.

"Jennifer," I called.

"Yes," she said immediately, responding with that quiet, deep voice of hers.

"Jennifer," I began again. "I — uh — I — I — feel—"

She interrupted me. "Sh! Don't say anything." She sat up in her bed. The moonlight, now pouring through the window, bathed her. Her silky pajama top was clasped together only at the midpoint of her chest. It fell wispily over her breasts, two silhouettes of languid flesh. Her movement shot a scent of her through the air, wafting over me.

"Come here," she commanded, her voice still soft and low. I threw my covers off and within moments found myself sitting on her bed. Our faces were now only inches apart. She slowly raised her hands and firmly, but gently, grasped my face in them. She looked deeply into my eyes. Pulling my face toward hers, slowly, she brought our lips together. The sensation of her lips brought me into another consciousness. I sank into her. Everything turned into a blur around me. All that existed was our two bodies coming together — and that moment in time.

ε℘

"Whew! It's about time!" Nickie said, as she sat cross-legged on the bed, her fingers gripping a book in her lap. She looked up at me with relief in her face. "I've been waiting for these two to get into bed for the last hundred and fifty pages," she added in disgust. She held the book tightly, open to that spot, as if she was terrified she would lose her place.

"What do you expect, people jumping into bed on the first page?" I asked.

"That would be a nice change of pace," she said, thoughtfully. "You know, I must read every lesbian novel that's written, just to squeeze out the one or two sex scenes that's in them. What I'd like is a book that's more sex than novel."

"Oh, I don't know," I said cautiously. "I think that would be P.I."

"P.I.?" she asked.

"Yeah, Po-li-ti-cal-ly In-cor-rect," I said firmly and clearly.

"What's political about sex?" she argued. "Women love sex too."

"No," I said. "Women love Love."

"Sex!" she said.

"Love."

"Sex."

"Okay, Love and Sex," I said, beginning to give in.

"Sex and Love!" she said, finally and emphatically.

"Hey, I know," she said, excitedly. "Why don't you write an erotic book? You're a writer." She was bouncing on the bed now, all ignited about this idea she had for my life. She continued, "You've always wanted to be a novelist. How about being a Sexist?" Her face was now ablaze.

"Very funny," I mumbled, dismayed by her pun. "You mean you want me to write something like the sexual *Reader's Digest* of the Lesbian Nation?" I added sarcastically. "Oh, wait, a great story is forming in my mind. I can call it, 'My Most Unforgettable Genital.'"

She giggled gleefully. "Come on, let's think of a title for your lesbian erotica."

I could see her mind was whirling. "Okay," I agreed, getting into it now. We sat thinking.

It came to me. I knew what the title of my book would be. With conviction, I told Nickie. "'Rapture.'"

"'Rapture'?" she asked with a perplexed look. "Well, if you're going to get religious about it, how about 'The Second Coming'?"

"Okay," I chuckled. "That will be the sequel. After all, sex is a spiritual experience."

"Yeah," she said, "people call out 'Oh, God' all the time during it."

"Give me a break," I laughingly admonished her.

Nickie was completely tickled with the whole idea. "Oh, I can't wait," she said, bouncing again. "An erotic novel with sex starting on the first page."

"Not the first page," I informed her.

"The fifth page?" she asked hopefully.

After a few thoughtful moments, I looked at Nickie's eager, waiting face and said, "The Introduction."

1

When I arrived in New York, I knew why choosing nursing as a profession hadn't been a mistake. I came, broke and desperate, to the harrowing haven. But a hospital quickly hired me and gave me a place to live — no small feat in New York. To add to my good fortune, I found myself, with my newly acquired lesbian sexual identity, surrounded by women. There, in a hospital huge enough to incorporate six city blocks, I worked with women of all shapes, sizes, ethnicity, ages, classes, and statuses.

Frightened, confused, and hurt deeply by my first woman lover, left two thousand miles behind, I had no recourse but to immediately fall in love with my head nurse, who exemplified everything I wanted to be. My lover had been a wretched alcoholic, and our relationship had been both passionate and horrible. Janey was exactly the opposite.

She had a ruddy kind of beauty. Her cheeks were pink and full, her body was small and hard with athletically powerful legs. Her eyes were large, brown, clear, and sharp. And I loved her salt-and-pepper hair, cut short, always neat and well groomed. Her lips fully and frequently held a friendly smile. She appeared to be in her early thirties although I suspected she might be older.

Janey radiated both physical health and mental stability; she loved the opera and ballet, ran marathons, and traveled. She had a sound knowledge of our field of psychiatry and, above all, seemed mature as hell. With my combined psyche of desperation, loneliness, and the exhilaration of a newly found sexuality, I wasted no time in going for it. My plan was, of course, to become her friend, to win her over through intimacy, and then to show her love she had never before experienced. I was quite sure she was a lesbian at heart, although during the first few weeks she frustrated me when she talked only of men. Yet somehow I knew I could safely and cautiously proceed. It was the looks and small flirtatious comments that gave me courage.

I courted and waited and was as wonderful as I knew how to be. Time crept by as I became more and more anxious about her seeming lack of interest in spending real time with me alone. She had too many goddamned friends!

But, finally! Out of the blue, patience paid off. She asked me out to lunch one day. We often had lunch together, but it never seemed to occur to her to make other plans with me. This time was different.

"Gwen, have you ever been to a concert in the park?" she asked, as we chomped down our food in a little coffee shop near the hospital.

"No," I answered, and a shiver ran through me. "I've been meaning to go. I've heard they're really nice."

"Oh, they're great!" she responded with enthusiasm. "You've got to go. I think they're one of the best things about summer in the city. Hey, you know what?" she continued, bubbling over, "there's a concert tonight. It's a good one too, the philharmonic. Want to go with me? I'd love to be the first person to show you this." She looked at me, waiting for an answer, smiling and chewing at the same time.

Trying to hide my overpowering excitement, I hesitated a moment. Then, nonchalantly, I said, "Yeah, okay, that sounds nice. I could go tonight."

"Great! You'll love it, I promise," she said, confirming our plans.

My big chance! I planned my strategy well. Although she was basically a non-drinker, a little bottle of wine in the park would give us both strength, not too much, but just enough ... then back to her place...

Arriving at the park, we settled into our little space on the great expanse of lawn amidst the festival crowd. I found it hard to believe that such a vast space could be so packed with people. Even so close together, they seemed to manage some elaborate dining out by candlelight on spread blankets. The evening was cool. Buildings surrounding the green wooded park loomed up majestically; they were like artificial mountains sparkling with electricity against the darkening pink-blue sky. As we arranged our own area, I was taken by the excitement and romance of it all. What a perfect place for courting, I thought.

Sitting, Janey plopped herself down close to me on the blanket. As we poured and sipped our wine, she leaned over towards me, pressing against my arm, every now and then touching me with her hand when she spoke. We mutually moved our heads close to each other to facilitate hearing each other's words and to play out the intimacy in the air around us. The effect of the wine was just as I expected. She loosened up, becoming more open and affectionate. We swooned with the flow of the music.

When the concert was over, she suggested we go back to her apartment for a cup of coffee. We strolled through and then out of the park, still carrying with us the enchantment of the evening.

As we sat in her apartment, she on the couch and I in a chair nearby, I told her how much her friendship had meant to me. She told me how wonderful it was for her to spend time with someone she could really talk to, someone who shared her vocational and personal interests. I told her I thought she was beautiful. She said she was experiencing something with me that was strange, but she couldn't quite describe what this feeling was.

I moved over to the couch. I took her hand and remarked how beautiful it was, stroking it with my other hand. Then, I touched her face softly, lightly caressing her eyelids and her mouth. Holding her face gently with both hands, I kissed her mouth. She moved forward and parted her lips slightly. I kissed her closed eyes and face and moved back to her lips with more intensity, sliding my tongue into her mouth. I felt her teeth and pressed and massaged her tongue. Then, with force, it came into my mouth and I sucked it. I felt her breasts, firm and small, with nipples hard. Lifting her t-shirt, I slid down and sucked her breasts, taking the whole in my mouth, then concentrating on the nipples. She moved and moaned and drew herself closer, spreading her legs slightly. While my mouth was absorbed with her breasts, I moved my hand down, unbuttoning her shorts, and slid it to her wet and warm crotch. I softly slid my fingers over and around her clitoris. Her moaning became louder and her legs spread wide. I felt my own wetness, and her moans seemed only slightly louder than the pounding of my heart. I was going to burst. I wanted to taste her — to fuck her with my tongue.

Quickly I drew off her shorts and moved my mouth down her belly to her clitoris, stroking it full force with the whole of my tongue. I thrust my tongue into her vagina and simultaneously licked and fucked. Her moans grew louder and she began gasping and exhaling air with force. Her spread legs began to tremble. I moved my fingers into her. She thrust her pelvis in rhythm to the penetration of my fingers. Suddenly she yelled out and shook violently for what seemed to be a long time but that, even so, ended too quickly. My face soaked, I kissed the inside of her thighs while she repeatedly twitched, then came to rest. We made love many times that night. Although timid in her approach to me at first, she soon became as expressive as she was responsive.

Exhausted, the next day we dragged ourselves to work and experienced that wonderful tiredness that comes from a night of lovemaking. It was fun carrying out professional duties with that particular air all the while tickling inside, feeling like someone had just made you queen of the planet.

Several weeks went by with life a blissful and beautiful game. It was all so easy. I felt strong and able to accomplish anything I wanted. Then, horribly, I began to experience the pain of her pulling away, the sense that she wasn't completely present when we were together, followed by her periodic suggestions that some space would be advisable.

Finally, the inevitable happened. She told me in tears how strongly she felt, but she couldn't accept the idea of a lesbian lifestyle. There was also something about the intensity and intimacy. In shock I listened. It was as if all of my nerve endings had just been short-circuited.

I lived in this state of shock, interspersed with denial and disbelief, for several weeks. Seeing Janey at work was torture. I suffered especially with the knowledge that eventually I would have to deal with the reality that she was again seeing men. I began fumbling through my life — groping around in the dark. Life was miserable with no hope. I had been cut down in my prime.

During the weeks that followed, waves of despair, denial, and anger welled up. A familiar hole opened up again inside my being, large and gaping. I started having delusions; I thought little things I experienced such as my horoscope or the message in a fortune cookie were signs from God that we would inevitably get back together. After all, isn't that what God wanted? Wasn't this relationship ordained by God? It had been perfect and I deserved it. I thought life went that way. You worked hard, suffered, struggled, and then you won. But I was losing again; how could this be?

It was at lunch one day that I began to get my revenge. A friend and colleague of mine who was also a lesbian began to fill me in on the facts of life.

"Don't go fucking around with straight women, Gwen, they're nothing but trouble. You never know where they stand. Yeah, it's true we all have to start somewhere, but there are some like Janey who have to put a lot of people through pain before they figure it out. It's a lot safer to stick with women who've been around in the community. And what a community it is! What you need is to find it. Why don't you come with me tonight? I'm going to the Princess; that's where you'll find women who know what they want. At least they know they want to sleep with women, and that's a start in the right direction."

I listened and believed.

❧ 2

*T*hat night Hope and I went to the Princess, a hot and crowded lesbian bar in the Village. I couldn't believe my eyes — all those lesbians in one place. I knew I had died and gone to heaven. Frightened and in awe, I stared for several hours, closing my mouth only to pour down another drink. The combination of booze, loud music, and hundreds of lesbians bumping and grinding began to diminish my pain. The butches were remarkable, the femmes gorgeous, and the androgynous women most fascinating.

Although I must have been quite unattractive as I sat wide-eyed and mouth agape, I noticed that a waitress seemed to be cruising me. (I determined that frequent, knowing, lengthy stares constituted cruising.) She was a beautiful, dark, heavy butch number, flat-chested, with greased-back, short dark hair, a tight muscle t-shirt, and hip-hugger jeans. Although mannish in appearance, she had a wonderful smile that softened her amazingly. I was immediately attracted to her strong and confident essence. It took a while, but finally, while taking another order for a round, she started to make jokes that seemed directed toward me. I responded weakly at first but managed to do what was necessary to encourage more. And then, wonderfully, while I was dancing, she came up close behind me, tray in hand, and whispered, "Meet me downstairs by the bathroom."

Great, I thought. *She wants to set up a date.*

Trying not to be too obvious, I excused myself from my dance partner and slid downstairs to the entrance to the bathroom. The stairway and bathroom were crowded and I thought, *How can we talk here?*

Shortly, my waitress appeared and stepped in behind me in line. She softly began to caress my hips and butt suggestively but discreetly. I said, "Hi," but she just smiled and continued to stand there quietly. When my turn came to go into one of the toilet stalls, my waitress nudged me slightly forward and we both slipped into the stall.

I laughed uneasily, turning to face her, and she kissed me hard and passionately. Then, while tonguing my ear, she whispered, "I'm sorry this will have to be quick; I don't have much time." My uneasiness gave way to excitement. My whole body tingled. A hot shudder flashed from my head down my belly to my genitals. I began to respond, rubbing my crotch against her leg as she pulled me closer, kneading my butt. I was soaked.

When she magically opened my blouse and began sucking my breasts, all the while rubbing and grinding my clit with her leg, I thought I was going to come on the spot. I grabbed the back of her head with both hands, forcing my breast still farther into her mouth and throat. As magically as with the blouse, she slid down my shorts and underpants. I spread my legs and began riding her bent knee. She wasted no time and plunged her fingers into my dripping vagina, moving them in and out and over my clitoris.

Then, with sopping fingers, she began to caress my anus, spreading my buttocks wide open with the other hand. She slowly and methodically nudged one finger into my tight hole. The initial strange feeling led to a most intense sensation, as if the whole lower portion of my body were being tickled inside. I had the urge both to laugh and to beg for more, which is what I did. She bent down on her knees and began sucking my clitoris, now shoving two fingers into my rectum. My whole bottom part was throbbing as I writhed. "Building ... heat ... coming...!" Then, orgasm burst forth. I stifled with great difficulty and not great success the scream that was in me.

We were both still, with her head buried in my crotch for a moment. She then got up, quickly kissed my mouth, smiled, and said, "I've got to go." Moments later, embarrassed to the gills, we emerged from the toilet, in some semblance of order, to face the crowd.

❧ 3

From that night on, I was hooked on the bars. Although most nights were not as arousing as the first, I loved the music, the women. Ah, the lesbians! I felt affirmed, that my life was exciting and wonderful. A special rush would come over me as I went through those doors, a rush that would settle into a normal high throughout the evening. One-night stands, the your-place-or-mine syndrome, didn't fill that empty place inside me, but for the moment they sufficed to reduce my consciousness of it. For many weeks, I explored every lesbian bar and disco I could find. I became the expert. Friends came to me for directions and advice on what the hottest place was — the best place to dance, where the most-gorgeous women were, the after-hours clubs. For a while I was satisfied.

Then, one night at Raspberry's, I sat talking with some new friends (they were always new). They told me about an interesting evening they had spent at the Gay and Lesbian Service Center. They said it was an organization that provided many kinds of activities: group counseling, discussions on the latest issues and books, musical performances, and even spiritual and meditative activities. I became curious. I was beginning to tire of the sameness of the bar scene. That aching void was getting larger and more difficult to subdue. Perhaps some sort of healing and artistic environment would be helpful. And, who knows, maybe the woman of my dreams would be there.

I made a decision. I would cut down on my bar activity. One of my friends said there was going to be a large meditation meeting that Friday night with music afterwards. I decided to go.

On Friday I walked into a huge and somewhat disheveled building in Chelsea. Getting momentarily lost, I finally arrived at the place where the meditation was beginning. It was a huge auditorium filled with about two hundred gay men and lesbians. Initially aghast to find men there, I suddenly realized that we were in fact united in our struggle — we shared many of the same concerns and much of the same despair.

Sitting down on the floor in the back, I weakly participated in some preparatory singing. Then a woman stood up in front of us. She was small, with wispy light hair and a sweet lilting voice. She looked almost childlike — too young to be in a position of spiritual leadership. Yet there was a quality of agelessness about her too, as if she had an old soul. Initially her presence was unassuming, interesting but subtle. She spoke about the meditation she was about to lead, and how she hoped it would enable us to open ourselves to ourselves and each other. She then led us through a meditation, her whole essence soft and caring.

I soon realized that I was opening, not necessarily to myself or others, but to her. By the end of the long prayerful evening, I knew I had been smitten by the most absorbing and consuming emotional and physical desire I had ever felt for any woman. For the first time in many, many months, an incredible warmth filled my deep inner void.

"Who is this woman?" I asked myself.

"She is the most wonderful being I have ever seen," I answered.

"What must I do to know her?" I asked.

"Pull together every thread of guile, lies, truth, goodness, mystery, sensuality, caring, passion, sincerity, unscrupulousness, wanting, needing, giving that is in me," I answered. In other words, do whatever it takes.

I approached her after the meeting and, after waiting my turn, introduced myself. She was warm and kind, her green eyes wide and innocent. But there was an uneasiness about her, a sense of distance. I felt distressed by this, but dismissed it, telling myself it was her own self-protection. As far as I was concerned, she was obviously taken with me.

I began to attend these meditations every Friday. Soon I learned that this wonderful woman was the director of the center. She was a psychologist who specialized in healing through spiritual and cosmic influences. She taught the concept of a power greater than ourselves to whom conflicts could be turned over in order to soothe psychic distress. Her name was Sarah.

I was obsessed. Nothing could stop me now. I was going to be Sarah's lifetime lover. All of the searching was over. I would fill up my life with her. As a thirsting person falls upon an oasis, I fell on her.

Awkward and stumbling, I approached her one night after a meeting. I thought my insides would burst if I didn't let flow the feelings pushing up through my throat. As I trembled and paced, I told her how I felt.

"Sarah," I blurted out, my voice shaking. "I'm in love with you." I paused and searched her face for a moment. It betrayed nothing. Her eyes were clear and open wide. She seemed to be waiting for me to continue.

"I seem to have developed this insatiable need for you," I went on, courageously. "I know this must all sound incredible. I can only tell you that my feelings are quite real."

She was kind. She said there was nothing wrong with my feelings. She took time with me and spoke softly as I began to calm down. She then explained that perhaps the intensity I felt for her was based on a need that would have to be met by an inner resolution. When I persistently argued and assured her that she was all I needed, she finally explained the facts. She had a lover she was very happy with. It was a monogamous relationship which she hoped and expected would be very long-term.

I was stunned. A lover! I'd never thought of that. In my excitement and insane obsession, I hadn't even considered this obvious possibility. Hopes dashed, I slithered home. There, when consciousness returned and reality set in again, I resolved to plunge forward, but more cautiously this time. I would fight for my beloved.

≈4

Normal life resumed. I began to get involved in many aspects of the center's operations. My feelings for Sarah were unchanged — just to be near her provided exhilaration — but I resolved to settle — for now — for a friendship. As time went on, however, that old longing began to make itself known again.

Attending the music events at the center became one of my favorite activities. There, surrounded by lesbians, I could listen to good music performed by other women of all levels of expertise. It was a good situation in which to meet other people, to begin to develop friendships, and, of course, to cruise. Outwardly, it was a civil environment, but underlying was the ever-present boiling of mutual desire. There, with relative ease, one could pursue another under the guise of social amiability. It was a pleasant change from the rawness of the bars, and I found the subtleties in many ways easier to deal with.

It wasn't long before I noticed a woman who attended these music events frequently. She was a great lover of many kinds of music, a pleasant and friendly person with a manner that seemed to exude sincerity. But most important to me was her quiet sensuality. She didn't writhe or wiggle or drip! She would merely stand close, smile, and look at me so intensely that she seemed to be looking through my eyes into my brain. She had a beautiful full mouth, a round face, beautiful soft curly dark hair, and a full firm physique. She dressed herself with a knowledge of what was most fitting and attractive for her; she had a professional air but with a little flair. Her aura was of innocence and openness. Although I still had Sarah constantly on my mind, I couldn't help but be attracted to this luscious creature.

I found out that Fran loved the beach. So did I. As summer was coming to a close, I thought what a perfect way to get to know each other — a day at the beach. One night during the social after the music performance, I asked if she wanted to hit the beach the following weekend with me. She said yes.

Saturday morning Fran picked me up in her car and we headed for Jones Beach. We both had packed ample fruits, cheeses, and juices to get us through that blistering hot early September day.

We had both heard of a gay section at Jones Beach but neither knew where it was. We picked out a couple of men who looked gay and cautiously asked if they knew. They pointed left and said it was way down. We walked and walked until we finally came to a place that was relatively secluded. Thinking this might be it, we parked ourselves. The sun was bright and unrelenting, without a cloud in the sky. We lay on the blanket, talking and laughing, intermittently swimming to cool off.

Whether it was coming from the intense heat of the day or from within myself I could not determine, but all I knew was that I couldn't seem to get very cool. Toward late afternoon we noticed that the beach was becoming more and more secluded. But neither of us made any move to leave.

I watched the beads of sweat as they continuously formed on her. Suddenly and without warning, she said, "I wish we were all alone here so I could make love to you."

Startled, I didn't know how to reply. After a few moments I began to softly and discreetly play with those beads of sweat on her arms and legs with my fingertips. She murmured as my fingers touched the nape of her neck and her back. I implored to the heavens at that moment that the few remaining beachers would go away. I thought briefly that we could leave ourselves, but I felt riveted to that place in the sand. I felt as if a magical spell bound us to where we were.

She reached out her hand and touched my face, staring into my brain as was her way. I was sure she was the most vibrant, sexual woman I had ever been with. Her sensuality seemed to be coming out of her pores like the moisture.

I moved closer, lying on my side facing her, and our bodies touched. When I could break my eyes away from her, I periodically checked out our neighbors. An older man and a little boy persisted. Facing each other, we lay, occasionally touching, caressing a body part. As the heat beat down, I thought I could see her body pulsating in rhythm with it. Water from her body was dripping between her breasts.

Glancing up, I saw that we were alone. Finally! The sun touched the horizon. I slid down slightly and ran my tongue into the crevice, following the sweat and retrieving it. She looked up and acknowledged our aloneness. Continuing to drink the beads on her shoulders and neck, I removed her bathing suit top. She in turn removed mine — as well as both our bottoms.

We lay on our sides, facing each other. We kissed — lips, face, ears, hair. I slipped my leg in between hers. We lay still for several minutes, the only movement being my upper thigh as it stroked her genitals.

Soon she began to move her pelvis more and more dramatically, sliding herself over my leg. Though she pressed her legs tightly, the lubricant of our sweat-bathed bodies provided the oil for free movement. I rolled on top of her. Our pelvises rode over each other, our bodies flowed together. As I leaned up and forward, she took my hanging breast in her mouth and sucked violently. Her hand reached between us and began to stroke my clitoris. The touch of her finger sent my raging body into spasms. I came. Then again. In a frenzy I turned and dove my head into her crotch, sucking and licking every membrane. She pulled my elevated pelvis, poised over her head, down onto her face and massaged my clit with her tongue. We ate each other voraciously. I burst again.

Then suddenly her legs stiffened; her pelvis under my mouth rose as she cried out and shook, withdrawing from my body for a moment only to return with more intensity, pulling at my butt and sucking me. Again I writhed and trembled; my bent, shaking legs threatened to buckle. My whole bottom half felt about to shake off the rest of me. Again her pelvis rose and her legs stiffened and jerked. The sweat poured and dripped off us onto the soaking blanket. We came again and again until in exhaustion we lay in silence, our heads submerged in the sweet pools of our life-giving fluids.

❧5

As we drove home that day, I felt a certain peace. Perhaps I had found the perfect woman. We had so many interests in common, we talked easily and well together, and most importantly, she was an incredible turn-on. Yet within me persisted a gnawing sensation that I couldn't quite define. For the time, I found it easier to put it aside. If I felt anything was lacking, I refused to acknowledge it.

Fran and I started to see each other regularly. We spent much of the fall attending concerts and events at the center; we even started to make some mutual friends as a couple. Spending time with other lesbian couples was a first for me. I had spent much of my time with lovers in isolation because my previous relationships had been shrouded in secrecy. Being able to be a couple openly in the community was comforting and enriching. I felt a sense of belonging. There was a different emphasis on life. Although admittedly I never stopped looking, I didn't feel so driven to find sexual partners. I was able to spend more time involving myself in productive and rewarding activities for the joy of them. I was able to start concentrating a little more on friendships.

One person I began to establish a friendship with was Sarah. My relationship with Fran relaxed the tension I had previously felt with Sarah. She became more willing to spend time with me alone. There seemed to be more openness between us. She clearly felt more at ease knowing I was in a relationship. For whatever reason, she now seemed more available for talks in her office or lunches at the Comet, a popular gay and lesbian restaurant near the center.

It was at the Comet that I first talked to her about my relationship. She knew Fran slightly from her visits to the music group. Expecting Sarah to be as enthusiastic as I was, I was surprised by her somewhat strained response. She said she was very glad for me, but her face was serious and sad. Could it be that she was not totally happy that I was involved? My need to talk to someone about my feelings, however, pushed me to confide.

As I began to relate the details of my so-perfect relationship, I began to get in touch with that pressing, gnawing feeling I had about Fran. As much as everything seemed to be there that should be, I wasn't quite sure that I was in love with her. Perhaps it was the ambivalence I felt from Sarah that gave me courage to explore this possibility. I wanted so much to be in love that I was trying to make it happen. I enjoyed the quiet sane sense of a relationship. I needed a rest. But I had to admit that I wasn't able to give myself over to this woman completely.

As Sarah and I began to spend more time together, I grew more acutely aware that my feeling for her hadn't changed. An inner battle ensued. As much as I wanted to force myself into love with Fran, I wanted to force myself out of love with Sarah. My initial readiness to go all out for her had been diminished by the pain of knowing she might never want me as a lover, and by the pleasure of becoming her friend. I still felt that wonderful sense of joy when I was near her. I didn't want to lose what I had in friendship by pressuring her and making both of us uncomfortable.

Having such an investment in holding back, I was able to accomplish an easy, more relaxed rapport with Sarah. She, in turn, cautiously opened herself to me. She talked of her fears and difficulties concerning the center and her role in it. Occasionally, she talked to me about her relationship. Sensing that it was hard for her to talk about this area of her life, I enjoyed to the utmost the times when she did. I felt privileged and thought that she trusted me most during these times. I also had to admit to myself a certain hope when I heard about difficulties in her relationship. *Oh, damn, why don't you solve all of our problems and dump that woman and be mine*, I would think. But I never said it.

❧ 6

Fran and I decided to go to Provincetown for a two-day camping trip. I was excited at the prospect of seeing the gay vacation capital of the world. I imagined lesbians and gay men falling all over one another in the streets and at the beaches.

We arrived on a cool October day. The streets were almost empty and the beaches were desolate except for a few people walking along the shore. I was disappointed also in the tourist population. Another fantasy down the drain — polyester suits reigned. Of those that were there, Mom, Dad, and the kids seemed to prevail. Fran and I still managed to be open with each other, holding hands and kissing occasionally out in public. But after my first grand imaginings were dissipated, I realized after some more vigilant inspection that the gay population was in fact definitely intact.

The first campground we went to had a sign: Families Only. Questioning the manager, we were told that same-sex partners were not allowed to camp on the grounds. I thought, well, we must be here for sure if they're so afraid of us. Finally we did find a nice camping area that allowed sodomites, and we moved our tent in for the weekend.

Fran had a roomy blue A-frame tent which we pitched in a soft green area surrounded by shrub pines. The area was relatively deserted since it was so late in the season. Only a few stout souls were braving October weather in the out-of-doors. We were delighted with our plight. The thought of bundling up together in sleeping bags with a campfire was enchanting. And I knew that, so far, I had never been cold with Fran.

After spending most of the day in town, topping it off with seafood and a swing on the dance floor at the lesbian bar, Fran and I returned to our home in the woods. We built a fire and sat by it, warming ourselves, huddled under a sleeping bag. I felt amazingly free being in this gay place with the added desolation of our campsite urging us to let go, to unleash, to let nature have its way. Since I also wanted to see and experience Fran's whole body, unshackled by any restraints of the elements, I compromised and we went into the tent.

Once inside, we giggled as I tore through the layers of her clothes. I pulled off one sweater, then the shirt, then the undershirt. She lay back as I pulled off boots, socks, jeans, and long johns. As the last thread of clothing came off, we both became gravely serious. She lay spread-eagled on the floor of our wilderness tent, and I was overcome with a savage desire for her.

As I knelt, rapt, caught for a moment in my own rush of wild passion, she broke the silence. "I thought this might be a nice time to try something we haven't done yet."

Still absorbed, I looked up.

She pulled out of her backpack a large pink vibrator. I was amazed at the way that our minds met, that she seemed to know how much I wanted to fuck her, to be inside her, to fill her completely.

I threw off my clothes and slid on top of her, both of us perfectly still. We were breathing in rhythm and I could hear the whoosh of air from her mouth in my ear. Her body was warm and the area where we touched seemed to bristle.

Clasping the vibrator, I slowly edged down to her feet, licking and kissing her whole body. Once at her feet, I turned on the long pink machine and started to massage her toes and the bottoms of her feet. She squirmed and we laughed. Slowly I edged my way up to the tops of her feet, to her calves and shin bone. I spent time on her knees. She began to move and make quiet growling noises. I ran it behind her knees and up the outside of her thighs, up her sides, into her armpits. Again the moving and deep quiet laughter. Then to her breasts, around the nipples first, and then on her nipples themselves, now firm and erect, around and over them until her whole body was in motion, squirming, her hands caressing my back.

I straddled her torso while continuing to vibrate her breasts. Her trunk arched up and my own wet cunt ground into it. Her sounds became louder, no longer laughing, but groaning. She said, "Now, please, put it in now." I moved the vibrator down the middle of her belly and circled her mound. Over her vaginal opening and her clit, around and around.

She began to moan loudly, "Please ... oh, please ...," her liquid flowing, wetting the pulsating plastic.

I thrust it gently into her canal. She jerked and yelped, then moved in rhythm with the in-and-out motion. I watched her writhe, her torso squirm, her legs tremble. She grabbed my head and my shoulders, sat up halfway, then fell back down, pulling at me. Her noises became louder over the sound of the buzzing and sucking dildo. As she shrieked and clung to my head, her orgasm welled up and her body began to go into spasms and jerk, her pelvis twitching.

My whole being throbbed. Fluid bubbled out of me. I had an intense craving: I wanted never to stop this immensely exciting rocking and fucking. But there was something else. While continuing to plunge into her with more and more intensity, my own insides flashing with waves of immense desire, I looked around the tent.

There, in a bag of fruit, was my answer. I grabbed at it and pulled out a hard banana. Peeling it partially, I quickly replaced the machine with nature's own. I thrust the softer substance into her again and again, harder and harder. I rode her, I galloped her, fruit joining come, smearing, sliding. I began to lick the fruit from around her hole and sucked her clit while continuing to plunge. Her body moved wildly. She yelled and shuddered again.

At this moment, my lower part, swelling, threatening to burst, with my mouth full of cunt and fruit, exploded, sending flashes through every part of me. I screamed and shook.

Melting together, we lay entangled, shivering, the pounding of her heart resounding through her belly into my soul.

&7

Fran and I left Provincetown exhausted and elated about our own personal discoveries and about our geographic find. I felt affirmed by being in a town so gay, so lesbian. Even with the polyester suits flying around I knew before we left that many of them came at least partly just to look at us: This was our place.

On the drive back we spent much time talking about what the trip had meant to us. It was during our discussion that a feeling of panic began to come over me. That sensation of uncertainty about the relationship would probably have been more subdued after such a weekend were it not for the fact that Fran began to push the issue a little. I didn't blame her at all for wanting to know where we stood, as I had become very good at avoiding the topic with her. In all respects it was probably time to put it out on the table. But I was unprepared. I wanted just to lap up the glorious weekend and not deal with reality. That was probably in part because I didn't know what reality was for us. Fran said bluntly that she wanted to pursue a monogamous relationship. She could not tolerate the thought of my sleeping with anyone else. Feeling the walls closing in, I explained that I wasn't sure I was ready for this step and that I would have to give it some thought.

Unhappily she said, "Okay, but I want to talk about it some more, soon."

Arriving back in the city, I immediately called Sarah and asked if we could meet for dinner the following evening. We made a date. During our brief phone conversation I was immediately aware of how much I had missed her even though it had only been a few days. I longed to look into those wide green eyes. At any rate, I told myself that this was a practical call. I needed someone to hash out my feelings with, someone who could give me advice. Sarah was the wisest person I knew. She always seemed to hear what I didn't say.

At dinner the next evening I told Sarah about the exciting realization of Provincetown. She commented on how the whole world could be that way if we could love each other instead of fearing each other.

She said, "Gwen, I feel so good when I'm in a place like that or even the Village here. But I feel so sad, so-o-o sad, when I think of how it could be like that everywhere. You know what I think? Sometimes I think we were put on this planet along with the other castaways to force others to grow. We're such a problem for them; they have to deal with us. That's why I think we have to be and are a particularly strong and beautiful people. When I look at geraniums, I think of lesbians: bright and colorful but with strong, thick leaves and roots. Either we're strong or we don't survive. It's one way or the other."

I sat and listened dreamily. When it came time for the telling of my plight, Sarah listened completely. I talked about how I felt so strongly about Fran in some ways, how we got along so well, how everything seemed to be right, yet I just felt something was missing. I couldn't quite identify what it was, but I still had a longing that wasn't satisfied in this relationship.

After I stated my case, Sarah advised me, "I know how that feels. It's very uncomfortable when you realize that what you always thought would be perfect somehow isn't. It kind of shakes you up — you're not really sure where to go from here."

"Yeah, that's it," I said.

"But Gwen, I'm afraid there are no easy answers to this. You need to keep talking about it. As you illuminate more and more of all of this to yourself, you might find some clarity. I also feel sorry for Fran. Maybe if you ask her she'll be willing to give you a little time. But it'll be hard for her."

I believed Sarah but suspected I already kind of knew what the problem was. It was the same problem I had since the day I had met her. For me, no one would ever equal Sarah.

❧ 8

Fran and I had spent some time with another lesbian couple who frequented the center and we all had become friends. Thinking it might be helpful to talk to someone who knew Fran, I called them one night and asked if I could see them soon.

Stephanie answered the phone. Morgan was going to be away on business over the weekend but if I wouldn't mind talking to just her, I could come over Friday night for dinner. I jumped at the chance, since I thought it would be more helpful to talk to Stephanie alone anyway.

Friday night I arrived at Stephanie's door in Park Slope to be greeted by hordes of family members. Two grown sons, a sister and brother-in-law, a brother and his wife, and two small children were milling about. *Great,* I thought, *just what I need, an audience.* Picking up my dismay, Stephanie immediately said, "Don't worry, they're leaving, at least most of them. I'm taking care of my son Jerome and my nephew, but they go to bed early." Somewhat relieved, I tried to be sociable.

The house finally emptied, and Stephanie and the two boys and I sat down to dinner. Stephanie had a large dining room. The table was nicely set with cloth and candles. I was adjacent to Stephanie, who sat at the head of the table, and the two boys were left to slobber their dinners at the other end. Pointing to them, she said, "You can talk in front of them. They don't know what you're talking about; besides, they're in their own little world over there. Don't worry about a thing."

I related to Stephanie all the things I had told Sarah about my situation. I told her about my thoughts, feelings, and confusion, leaving out any references to Sarah. Stephanie was patient and serious, interjecting at times what she had observed when she had been with us together.

During our conversation, and particularly when we had gone onto lighter topics, I was keenly aware of Stephanie's beauty. I had always thought her beautiful from the moment I had first seen her at the center but had tried not to notice after the four of us began spending time together. I knew her relationship with Morgan was solid, and I did not consider myself a home wrecker. Now, in the candlelight, her clear dark brown skin glistened. I loved the way her hair — short, black, soft — perfectly rounded her face. Her eyes were clear and brown, her lips full. Her figure was perfectly formed with large firm breasts. She laughed easily and with enthusiasm. Her eyebrows knit together with annoyance when she scolded the boys. She appeared much younger than her thirty-eight years.

While I was busily trying to put all lustful desires out of my consciousness, Stephanie calmly stated, "You know that Morgan and I have an open relationship, don't you?"

"Uh, no, I didn't really know that," I said, trying to remain calm.

"God, I thought everybody knew. Well, I guess we don't exactly advertise it," she informed me.

"Well, are either of you seeing other people now?" I inquired.

"Presently I'm not, and I don't think Morgan is. We have an agreement not to discuss our comings and goings with each other," she offered.

The children giggled and played with their food at the end of the table, seemingly unaware of us.

"You know, I've always thought you were very beautiful," I said, thinking about what a jerk I was.

"Girl, you don't waste any time, do you?" she said with a chuckle. "But thanks. I've always been attracted to you, too, to be honest."

Losing myself, I said, "I'd like to make love to you." My heart was pounding as it always did when I made the move.

She laughed quietly. "I was hoping you would."

I slipped off my running shoes under the tablecloth. With a socked foot I began to feel the insides of her legs, running it along her inner thighs under her skirt. She laughed and said, "Oh, yeah," with emphasis on the 'yeah.' I removed the sock from my right foot and, following the same progression, delightedly discovered she was not wearing underpants. I stroked her pubic hairs, rubbed against her hole and inner thighs until I felt her wetness on my toes.

The kids continued, oblivious to us. She began to edge down on the chair, spreading her legs. I turned my chair toward her and began to work my big toe into her opening. She sighed and grunted, closing her eyes halfway, pushing herself closer to me. I worked my toe in and out of her slowly, wishing I could put my whole foot in there. The rocking movement aided that familiar feeling welling up in my own groin.

I pulled my toe all the way out and rubbed it up and down her labia. She drew in air quickly and before long said, "I'm going to put these kids to bed." Getting up weakly from the table, she removed and ordered the resistant children to bed. Although kicking and screaming, they seemed to know she meant business.

I went into her bedroom and promptly removed my clothes. When she breezed into the room, I drew her quietly onto the bed. Raising her skirt I immediately began voraciously eating her cunt. I sucked, licked, and gurgled while her pelvis gyrated. I stuck my tongue in her, tasting the sweetness. I alternated plunging and licking, plunging and sucking, smearing my whole face in her crotch. I slid my hands under her buttocks and spread them wide. Her breath came quickly, loudly, grunting in staccato rhythm. She jerked her pelvis rapidly up and down. She yelled out loud, her shimmering brown knees flailing. "Yes, yes!" she screamed, and exploded in orgasm.

Winded, breathing heavily, she came to rest. Then she removed her clothes and began to glide over my body, still face down on the bed. Her breasts caressed my back, butt, and legs. She turned me over and repeated this action all over my front. She played with my face, her beautiful breasts sliding in and out of my mouth. Then she began to lick me. Everywhere she licked me. Her tongue glided over my skin. I trembled in anticipation. Expertly finding my clitoris, she concentrated, she massaged me, bit me lightly. She teased me until I grabbed and pulled at her head with all my might. Then she went at me as if she were going to swallow me. Rocking wildly, I came with a burst of incredible intensity. As my body shuddered I lay bewildered in joyous amazement. I cradled Stephanie's head in my crotch for a long time.

Stephanie and I spent the whole weekend together. We made love in between her taking care of the kids. And we did manage to find the time to enjoy them. I was somewhat amazed at how I didn't hate being with them. And while they napped, we fucked. I felt intensely the wonderful abandon of a physical relationship with no commitment or expectation except that of the moment.

· Whether or not she knew it, Stephanie had helped me greatly in being able to come to a final conclusion about Fran and myself. As painful as it would be for both of us, I knew I could not commit myself to a monogamous permanent relationship with Fran. Knowing how she felt, and now how I felt, that meant breaking off.

I dreaded losing her. I was afraid of not having that one person there I knew loved me. I knew I couldn't have the freedom I needed to pursue that perfect person who was going to be my happiness if I stayed with Fran.

9

A week later Sarah and I sat on her stoop. "I made up my mind last weekend; I'm going to have to end it with Fran," I confided.

"Oh, I thought you were going to give it some time," she said, as a wave of pain ran across her face. I saw in her a sorrow of identification.

"You look sad," I said.

She said, "It's just that I think breaking up is one of the most painful things we have to endure. It incorporates so much. It's not that I don't think it's necessary at times, but it's never easy, no matter whether you're the rejecter or the rejectee, or if it's mutual. And it doesn't seem to matter how long the relationship has lasted. Sometimes the shortest ones can be the hardest to lose. I feel really bad for both of you. I remember when I cried every day one whole summer over a breakup. So far, that's been the worst experience of my life."

She dropped her head and studied the ground. We were silent for a few minutes. I thought that she was feeling not only for herself but for all of us at that moment. I both admired and was aghast at how Sarah seemed to take on the burden.

"When are you going to talk to her?" she asked.

"I don't know," I mused. "It will have to be soon, though. If I don't tell her, she'll have to deal with knowing the truth without being told, which is torture. I guess I'll have to let my intuition control the timing."

"Yeah, I think that's best," she assured me. She looked at me deeply and half smiled.

That night Fran and I attended a book discussion group at the center. Afterwards the group of women went to the Comet. Sitting near us there was another table full of older women from the senior citizens' lesbian group. It was invigorating watching them. I found myself wondering what life had been like for them years ago. I thought about how they had prepared the way for us — not without much struggle and tribulation, I was sure. Almost as if in answer to my musing, an ancient beauty said loudly to her fans, "I used to make out in a car parked on MacDougal Street, back in the days when you could really kiss the hell out of a girl."

Our table rocked with laughter. I was sure I could get a few tips on lovemaking from her.

Later, Fran and I decided to go to her place. Alone, our usual chatter was replaced by long periods of silence. As we sat in her living room, arms around each other, I felt a tremendous urge to forget all about my conclusions and just go on as it had been. The two sides of me were going at each other again.

After a while Fran cleared the way. "Is something going on with you? You seem a little preoccupied tonight."

I stared downward, silent for a moment. I sighed, and then, feeling as if someone were squeezing my chest, I said, "Yeah, there is. Uh, I've been thinking a lot about our relationship and what we talked about coming back from Provincetown. I think I need my freedom." *Oh, shit, I can't believe I'm such a jerk; why am I hurting her?* I screamed at myself inside.

She looked frightened and trembled almost unnoticeably. I told her all the things I had considered and how it had come to the point that as much as I cared for her, I wasn't willing to give myself over to this relationship. We talked and cried and spent the night in each other's arms like two lead weights. The urge to take it all back continuously welled up in me to the point of being almost unbearable, only to subside with a knowledge that the choice was not mine, but came from a need I could not control.

I spent the next several days isolated, deeply depressed. I drank heavily. I felt loneliness, despair, self-pity, self-hatred. *What is wrong with me?* I thought. *Why can't I just be happy? What am I looking for?*

I called Sarah and spoke to her not too clearly on the phone. I knew there wasn't much she could say, but I wanted to hear her voice. It was almost as if I needed some reassurance that she would be there for me. I was morose and wanted to find some external reason for my actions. In my stupor I could only find justification in myself through someone else. Somehow I knew it didn't quite make sense, but I allowed myself the luxury of feeling comforted by whatever means I chose.

*10

Fran had asked that we not see each other for a while. I decided that the music groups were out for me, and that in fact I should probably steer clear of the center for a few weeks, except for the meditations, which Fran didn't attend. I had two weeks of vacation coming, so I decided to go to Maine, where my best friend from college and her lover lived. I spent the rest of the week recuperating from my emotional and physical binges and then hopped the bus to Portland, Maine.

On the long ride I thought often about my decision to break up with Fran and began to feel a little better about it. I was looking forward to spending time with Teresa. We had been extremely close for years, but had only come out to each other a couple of years before. Although she had been having relationships with women longer than I, it was as though we had come out together. We understood each other completely; we had seen each other through many changes and traumas. I knew I would find relief in her insight and support. In my self-deprecating state it felt good to be going to see someone who loved me no matter how horrible and mixed-up I was.

Walking off the bus, I saw the radiant face of this wonderful being who was waiting for me. My pain diminished instantly, and we embraced for a long time. She held me knowingly. She didn't know the details of my currently miserable life, but she knew me well enough to intuit the place I was in.

"It was so good to see that red head bobbing off the bus," she exclaimed. We laughed at her effusiveness and began a stream of chatter as we related our recent life's events to each other. Being with Toss (a nickname she had acquired in college) gave me the same sense of being complete that being with Sarah did. Although my feelings about them differed, the end result felt very much the same. With Toss I had the sense of a complete, enduring, and lifelong love. Mutual identification, total acceptance, the letting down of all guises, and complete sharing were the bases of our friendship. Yep, we had been through it all together and fully expected to go through whatever was to come together as well.

Toss took me to dinner — lobster, of course — and we spent the evening and the next few days staying up all hours drinking in each other. Her lover, Sally, was visiting her family, and Toss, although glad to have the time alone with me, anxiously awaited her return. When Sally did return, I felt mixed emotions. I didn't know Sally too well and was glad to spend some time relating with the lover of my friend. But I was also jealous to be losing the complete attention of Toss. The first evening together was somewhat strained as we all had to take our places. Also there was a slightly disconcerting feeling of attraction I felt for Sally. I found her interesting and physically comely.

She was small in stature. She wore her dark hair very short and curly with a little tail in the back. She had the early stages of little lines in the corners of her eyes that aided an older persona. She dressed plainly, wearing a lot of jeans and flannel shirts. Yet her clothes were colorful and crisp even in their earthiness. Her small mouth and eyes frequently betrayed a mischievousness, an impulsiveness, a willingness to jump at any chance to have fun.

Toss, on the other hand, was soft in appearance and personality. She was heavyset with large breasts. She moved slowly and deliberately as if weighing her steps. Her words she also weighed, always thinking intently before letting them out. She wore her black hair long, often tying it up in the back. Her face was round and her eyes twinkled, always watching for something that would make her laugh.

It was getting quite cold in Maine already in November, and Toss and Sally had worked out their living situation according to where the heat was. They spent much of their time in the living room where the large wood stove was. They had a large sofa bed in there, and in the cold weather that's where they slept. They informed me that we would all be sleeping in one room. I was to take my place on a cot by the stove. I was glad for this as I really didn't want to be alone anyway.

The three of us talked well into the night. Sally told us all about the usual disastrous visit with her parents. I caught Sally up on my most recent misadventures. We laughed a lot and bore each other's sorrows. One by one we started to get ready for bed and to settle in for the night. As the lights went out and our talking subsided, I thought about how nice it was to be with people without sexual tension.

As I lay in my cot listening to the crackle of wood in the stove and the wind outside, I heard something else. Sally and Toss seemed restless and moved a lot. I disregarded it. Then it began to sound as if they had both just run five miles. Yep, it was heavy breathing all right ... and sucking noises. I immediately tried to cope with my uneasiness by thinking how interesting the situation was. *I'll look at it as if I were observing an experiment,* I decided.

To show how cool and indifferent I was I said, "Do we all get to smoke a cigarette after this?"

They giggled, were quiet for several minutes, then resumed. I heard quiet murmurings and some giggling. Still in an academic frame of mind, I said to myself, *Ah yes, the second stage of the Saphrodykic mating system.*

Suddenly, and without warning, two dykes swooped down on me from the blackness of the night. They lay on top of me, tickled me all over, and began to explore my body. We laughed uproariously, and I pleaded for mercy. They then scooped me up, one at my legs and one at my shoulders, and levitated me into their larger bed. We rolled around and wrestled, tickling and holding each other down, alternately exchanging comrades in arms.

Tired from the playful fighting, I finally lay back on the bed, still laughing in spurts. Looking up, I noticed the enemy sitting cross-legged, looking at me, the devil in their eyes.

Sally said, "You're pretty strong, such a nice wiry body. Umm, I like it." She began to touch my breasts gently, still with a smile but not laughing. Toss began to rub up and down my legs to my crotch and back down to my feet.

In a few moments, I said, "I don't know what you two think you're doing, but don't stop." I lay with my eyes closed, feeling goose bumps all over. They continued to softly massage me. Toss was now brushing my crotch over my underpants. Sally pushed up my t-shirt and began kissing and sucking my breasts.

I quickly moved into the place of no return. Still with my eyes closed, I spread my limbs wide and took in the pleasurable feelings. I felt moans coming from my throat and my body began to wriggle of its own accord. Toss plucked off my underpants and began to kiss my legs, upper thighs, and stomach. Sally continued to suckle my breasts, one, then the other. In my totally passive state I was completely in their hands.

Toss lifted my legs and spread them wide. She began to lick my inner part. I felt liquid running out of me down between my buttocks. My pelvis raised up, humping Toss's face. My back began to arch, shoving my breast further into Sally's mouth. Everything in me was rising. I tried to hold back, wanting to continue wallowing in the tide of pleasure. I tried to stop Toss, pushing at her head with my hands, but she was unrelenting.

Finally, I let go helplessly. The flow gushed over my body — stiffening, arching, rocking as the hot waves of pleasure shot throughout my flesh. I was on fire. Quickly Sally left my breasts and slid her wet space over my mouth. She spread her legs, one knee on either side of my head, her torso straight above me. Her lean, tight abdomen and small pointed breasts towered over me. I thrusted my tongue in and out of her canal, massaging the labia. I stroked her and lapped her whole cunt. I spread and kneaded her ass with my hands. She began to writhe and bounce on my face.

Toss continued to suck me and inserted her fingers in my vagina. I felt filled up. The rising began again. Sally's cunt was soaking, and the bouncing became more and more rapid.

She cried out loudly. Toss moaned, plunged, and sucked. I stuck my fingers into Sally. She began to force herself down on them. We pushed and pulled together. Toss's expert tongue and thrust brought the tide once more. Continuing to suck, I groaned and shook. At that moment, Sally pressed her cunt on my face hard, and grinding into me, she jerked. Then she hopped on my fingers in quick motions, her canal closing tightly on them. She gasped, grunted, and cried out in ecstasy.

Moments later Sally and I moved to Toss. I sucked Toss's huge breasts while Sally worked her over below. Toss, already steaming, moved wildly, her breasts slipping out of my mouth. I grabbed the voluptuous nippled orbs that loomed up at me, and held them tight, squeezing them into my mouth. She squirmed and then leaped, holding her body arched. She came, her liquid streaming.

Bathed in sweat, we lay entangled. Heavy in each other's arms, I thought, *Sally should have come home earlier.* We slept, surrounded by one another for the few remaining hours of the night.

Late in the morning we got up and Toss served a huge breakfast of omelettes, fresh blueberry muffins from her mother's kitchen, juices, and coffee. I felt a little strange at the breakfast table. My old inner tape, which played a tune about how one doesn't sleep with one's friends, was in no way going to fit with this situation. The sensation I was feeling was an incompatible mixture of things. On the one hand, I felt particularly close to both of them. And on the other hand, I almost didn't want to look into their eyes. Toss and I had been so close for so long that it seemed totally natural yet embarrassing, as any new intimacy usually is.

We talked mostly about mundane matters. I sensed that we would probably discuss all of this at some more distant point.

As they placed me on the bus, we all looked meaningfully at each other, embraced, kissed one last time, and bid our farewells. Riding back home, my perplexed feeling gave way to a certain calm. I felt more secure in our friendship than ever. Our fling had helped cement a bond between Toss and me, particularly since she was safely tucked away in a marriage and no tension as a result of our sexual encounter was likely.

While the bus hummed along toward the city, I began to think more about what I would do about my life once I got back. I felt more solid in my decision to break up with Fran and less miserable about it. I recognized for the first time how important friends were, and how one needn't feel alone just because one had no permanent lover. I was certain that a permanent relationship was not for me at this time, and I knew that I needed to rethink those lessons I had learned at my mother's knee — that marriage and commitment was the ultimate. Perhaps it was possible to have love and freedom after all.

My thoughts drifted to Sarah. A surge of happiness swept through me. Maybe I could be satisfied just being her friend. Maybe she would grow to love me in another way, if being lovers wasn't possible, that could still have much depth, meaning, and satisfaction. I wanted so much to be close to her.

Perhaps a short period of celibacy wouldn't be a bad idea in general, just to let my latest thoughts sink in. I didn't want to entangle myself in another confusing situation. Yes, I needed a dry period in which I could develop platonic love relationships. That was the answer for now.

≈ 11

*A*rriving at home, I put off calling Sarah for as long as I could, then had to give in. The answering machine was on. I fought with jealous impulses that told me she was out having a good time with someone else. I left a message that I had returned to town and that I would call tomorrow. Wanting to retain my positive outlook on my life, I pushed unhappiness aside and jumped into bed, ready to start back to work, new philosophy in hand, the next day.

I got up in the morning looking forward to my new life. I wasn't exactly anxious to go to work, but I felt confident of my desire to put more into my vocation. I would try to be there more for the patients and really start exerting my knowledge and ability. I'd try harder to rekindle a friendship with Janey and start looking at all the women more platonically and with less lust. I would free myself from the confinements of my sexual desire.

As I walked to the subway, the air was crisp and clear. The sun was just rising, softening slightly the barren, gray, winter environment of the city. I arrived at the platform with the other early morning rush-hour people. I was always amazed that in New York, rush hour seemed to start at 6 a.m. and last until almost noon.

The platform was crowded as the train pulled up. I saw that it was going to be one of those days when I had to cram myself into the car. I squeezed through the throng and pushed my way to the door that separates the cars, leaning my back against the door for support.

As the car started moving, I noticed standing close to me a very beautiful woman. She was slightly shorter than I, with a soft, full face, shoulder-length curly brown hair, and a body that wouldn't quit. She had gorgeous large breasts that stood out firmly. Wow! *Well, I can't help looking,* I thought.

Soon the train stopped to let out a few people and to take in even more. The woman got pushed in closer to me and was standing with her lovely bosom pushed up against my arm. I stiffened with embarrassment but also secretly felt delighted. The train moved on. I was immediately aware that the woman's breast rubbed up and down against me with the bouncing of the train. She smelled fresh from a morning shower and had on neat, clean clothes. Her hair radiated a flowery shampoo fragrance. I closed my eyes, felt her body moving against me, listened to the click-uh click-uh click-uh of the train. I was getting warm.

While absorbing the sensations, I felt her adjust her position. Opening my eyes, I saw her facing me squarely, our bodies shoved together, front to front. She looked at me and smiled slightly. My face must have reddened deeply, and I thought she sensed what I had been feeling.

Then I felt something on my outer thigh. She was touching me with her hand. Oh, glorious, wonderful life! I knew then that she probably *did* know my mind and had one like it. Subtly, I put my own hand over hers on my thigh and led it in toward my center. She caught her breath, inhaled long and deeply. Our two hands began to move up and down my zipper, dipping in between my legs. Still leaning against the door, I spread my legs a little more. We bounced with the movement of the train, and giggled. The sounds it made as it ran seemed to grow louder. She pressed her body hard against mine and continued to rub my crotch. Her breasts squished into me, the train movement causing them to rub and tease my own. My clit was titillated and extremely sensitive; I began to rock toward her, our bodies grinding together quietly. I felt my underpants getting wet.

The train came to another stop, tossing people about. The woman had been pushed away from me slightly. As everyone regained their balance, I spread my legs a little more, and she, amazingly, unzipped my pants and slipped her hand inside. With one movement, while pushing up against me again, she wiggled her fingers underneath the leg band of my underpants and we were flesh on flesh. She made a slight noise, exhaling air quickly, and I began to sweat and tingle all over. The train started up with a jolt, and she pressed her fingers hard against me. I jerked with the shot of pleasure that ran through me.

The train was moving smoothly again, and she kept her fingers held against my clit, the rest of her hand cupping my bush. As the train rocked us, her hand and body moved up and down, pressing and relaxing in rhythm. My pelvis throbbed. I felt the rush coming on. *Oh, please don't stop,* I thought. I began to tremble. My knees got weak. I wanted to pull her to me tightly and jump on her hand. Water dripped from my pits and brow. I struggled to stifle grunting noises that forced their way from my throat. My thrusting became more pronounced. Feeling rubbery, I held on to the door of the car with my hands. The noise of the moving train pounded in my skull.

Suddenly we screeched to a halt. At that moment, she pushed hard against me and moved her hand rapidly and with force against my saturated groin. A flash went through me. I shuddered all over, my legs and pelvis twitching. A hot sensation of mounting pleasure drained me. I clenched my teeth and groaned softly. Shivering, I caught myself from sliding to the floor.

As the train resumed its journey, she slowly removed her wet, shaking hand from me. I regained my composure and looked around us nonchalantly, trying to determine from people's faces whether or not they had noticed anything. Everyone seemed to be looking away or downward and gave no indication of interest in me and my friend. But I still knew some of them had to have seen it all. *Oh, well,* I thought, *I'll probably never see any of them again in my life.* The cynical part of me said, *Yeah, one of them will probably end up being my new nursing supervisor or something.*

I then gazed into my friend's eyes. They were dancing as she smiled and blushed. I wanted to say something but didn't know what. I was still trying to find words when the train stopped again. My subway lover was moving to get off. As she turned to leave, I grabbed her arm quickly and said, "Thank you."

She turned her head, smiled fully, and said, "Any time."

I dropped my hand from her arm, and she rushed out of our rumbling, crowded boudoir.

*12

*A*s I arrived at work, I was flustered and still flushed. I tried to absorb myself in tasks immediately, avoiding others, so that I could think. I sometimes could think best while making beds. While shaking and pulling sheets and putting in the hospital corners, I mused. Obviously, I thought, this new philosophy was not going to work. It was shattered already. *But what about my decision about platonic relationships and celibacy? Can't I still try it?* Maybe if I really put my mind to it I could be virginal as the pure driven snow.

As the day progressed, I realized that, try as I might, I simply was not able to turn off my body, which was stronger than my mind. I made a new resolution to stay out of trouble. I would stick to casual relationships. And I would be very clear about it.

During the day, I gave Sarah a call at the office. She answered and greeted me. "Gwen, I'm so glad you're back! Can we get together this evening? There's something I want to talk to you about."

"Of course," I said, as matter-of-factly as possible.

"Why don't you come by after work?"

"I'll be there at five," I said gleefully. Hanging up the phone, I felt light-bodied, as if I might rise off the chair. What could this be? I know: She's missed me terribly and has decided to dump her lover for me. *Wait a minute! Cool out, kid. It's probably something about the center,* I chided myself. From that moment, I waited in guarded anticipation for the hours to pass until our meeting.

I arrived at Sarah's office at five, and she welcomed me with a big hug and hustled me in. Enthusiastically, she said, "Something's come up that I think would be wonderful for you to work on here at the center."

"Oh?" I said, trying to hide my disappointment.

"One of our best counselors came up with the idea of a great group that would be very helpful to our women's community."

"What's the idea?" I said, my voice shaking.

"Well," she said, "It would be a support group of women in relationships; you know, about commitment and continuity. You would co-lead it with her."

"Sounds like the title of a book, *Commitment and Continuity*," I let slip out sarcastically.

"Come on, Gwen, it's a really good idea, don't you think?"

"Yeah, Sarah, it's a good idea, but what makes you think I know anything about that?"

"You don't have to be a master of the art to be able to help people get in touch with themselves and lend support. You just have to know group process. And you do. You do groups at work, don't you? And I know you could do it," she said persuasively.

Sarah's brightness and positive aura were always more than I could bear to turn down. I said, "Let me think about it. Oh, fuck — I'll do it." Little did she know I would do anything she asked.

"Good," she squealed. "It will be a good experience for you and great for the community. Let me give you Linda's telephone number.so you can talk it over with her."

❧13

That night I gave Linda a call. She was pleasant but business-like. Her deep voice was even, controlled, and serious. We made plans to have dinner the next day. After our precise and to-the-point conversation, I thought, *At least this will help keep me out of trouble, running a group of committed people with Ms. Business Machine.*

The next day at the appointed dinner hour, I was pleasantly surprised. Walking into Gerry's Salamander, a health-food restaurant, I looked around for someone who might be Linda. I spotted a woman sitting alone, wearing large glasses and a blazer and turtleneck. Must be her, I thought.

As I approached her, she said without smiling, "Hello, are you Gwen?"

"Yes, and obviously you're Linda," I said with a laugh.

"You're slightly late. Did you have trouble finding the place?" she asked.

I thought, *Oh, boy, rather, oh, girl, this is going to be a difficult relationship.* Sitting down across from her, I noticed that under the strictness of her attire was a beautiful woman. She had large clear blue eyes, high cheekbones, soft straight brown hair. Her face was perfectly chiseled, Nordic-like. Her teeth glistened white and straight. This might not be so bad after all.

During the course of the evening I became aware that my co-leader was not the least bit interested in anything but our project. We talked of personal matters only inasmuch as was necessary to facilitate leading the group. We talked about our own experiences, thoughts, and feelings about commitment. I was honest about my own confusion. Linda was undaunted and stated that many others would feel this way, too, and that we weren't selling a product, but trying to help others get in touch with things they had been frightened to acknowledge.

"We're trying to foster communication and let people know that their feelings are okay. People generally hide the things they think will threaten their relationships, not realizing that in staying hidden, these things are in reality more dangerous. They have a tendency to come out in perverted ways or build up to the point of explosion. That's what seems to happen in many of these outwardly stable long-term relationships that suddenly end without warning. At least, that's one aspect of it," she preached.

By the end of the evening I was convinced. Although still put off by Linda's serious, standoffish air, I was impressed by an underlying sense that this woman really did understand people. At least she was able to accept me with all my weirdness. There was a warmth underneath it all, a kind of I-love-woman humanity that had nothing to do with sex. I connected with an element in her that I had consciously been trying to elicit from myself. I sensed in her that she managed to accomplish what I had been seeking to do, to move the love from my crotch up a few inches to my heart. But my tunnel kept caving in. How was it that hers didn't? Maybe her tunnel went in the other direction. At any rate, it seemed quite clear that on a physical level neither of us was going to be excavating the other.

We decided to get together a couple more times in the following week to plan our group, and, in the meantime, to put up publicity posters at the center advertising it. We would admit ten women, each a spouse from a committed relationship. The group would last eight weeks. Linda and I would cram in some reading from a book on group process that we had chosen to help prepare ourselves. We would have pre-group and post-group sessions to plan and then discuss what went on each time.

In the next two weeks we had an overwhelming response to our ads and had to turn down many women. It was obvious Sarah was right about the need for this. Linda and I were well prepared, and when the first group session met, both of us saw and remarked on how well we worked together. The differences in our personalities complemented each other nicely. Her weaknesses were my strengths, and vice versa. By the second group session I admired her talents and was amazed to realize that she admired mine.

An unfortunate aspect, however, was a lingering annoyance she seemed to have regarding my language. She would call me, in our sessions, on my usage of sexist imagery and my lack of skill in utilizing inclusive language. I had no patience with this overly feminist preoccupation and argued that I felt I could use any language I wanted. I had been using it all my life. I thought that way. I couldn't help it.

When she wasn't overtly furious with me, she would try to explain: "Gwen, you just have to realize that women can't relate completely to the world of *man*kind. This comes from a patriarchal structure that has been blatantly set up to benefit men, not women." At the end of each spat, I would promise to try to think and talk from a feminist perspective.

Even though we continued to irritate each other, as time went on my respect and attraction to Linda grew. I wondered if this woman of such high standards would go to bed with me. And if she did, what would it be like to make love in a politically correct manner? I envisioned a sign above her bed: No dildoes allowed!

After the sixth group session, Linda and I decided to walk home and have our post-group meeting while walking. We discussed all that had happened during the group, how so-and-so was intellectualizing or being manipulative. We talked about how we handled the session and fielded the problems.

After exhausting the subject, we walked along in silence for a while. The air was cold and biting as we stepped at a brisk pace up Seventh Avenue towards Linda's upper West Side apartment. During our silence my mind raged with indecision and fear. Should I just be direct and ask if she wants to make love, or should I try the long courtship method?

Filled with a sense of urgency, I blurted out suddenly, "Would you consider going to bed with me?"

She walked on blank-faced, and said nothing. I couldn't read her, and for a few moments I thought I might die from embarrassment. I kept looking at her face, then to the ground, waiting painfully. For a second I wondered if she had heard me. Finally, she looked half at me and half off into space so that our eyes met only for an instant and said, "Yes, I would."

Again, silence. I wondered, *Now what? What do I do now? Should I make a date?*

Interrupting my thoughts, she began to talk. "There's just one concern of mine, Gwen. See, I don't plan on getting involved with anyone. I'm making a conscious effort to stay free from any commitments at this time in my life. You probably find this surprising — that I would be this way, I mean. I guess I sort of seem like the love-and-marriage type, but right now I'm trying to develop more intimate friendships and want to keep myself open without restraints. I would like to make love with you, but I want you to understand that that doesn't mean we're going out to buy furniture together next week."

She was right; I was surprised and slightly put off. But I rallied, and, while responding, realized that Linda had spoken the words of my own conscious mind.

I confided, "I respect your feelings a lot, and, in fact, I feel very much the same way. I've recently made a decision along those lines myself. Actually, if you look at the two of us, anyway, there's not much danger of us falling in love. I mean, we're so different."

She gave a laugh and said, "Yeah, that's true."

We walked on in silence again. It was getting cold and seemed about to snow. I was aware that my feet were frozen and hurting. "Well," I said, "how about if I give you a call? We could have dinner some night."

"What's wrong with tonight?" she ventured. "Come on; let's hop in a cab and go to my place."

"All right," I said, thinking, *There is life after feminism after all.*

☙14

Trying to flag down a cab was difficult; that phenomenon basic to New York life struck — just when you need a cab, there are none. We continued trudging in silence. Then Linda said, sticking out a gloved hand, "Would you hold my hand?"

"Out in public?" I croaked.

"Yes, I'd like you to hold my hand," she responded firmly.

"Uh, well, we're sort of close to my job, but ... okay, I guess."

We walked along, my arm extended rigidly, holding hands. As I was barely getting used to my discomfort, Linda proceeded, "Would you put your arm around me?"

This was going a little too far. I laughed nervously and said, "Put my arm around you? Right here?"

"Yes, what's wrong with right here?" she argued.

"Look, Linda, I'm just not comfortable doing that in public. People will look at us. Look where we are. What if we run into somebody from my job?" I stood up for myself, knowing she would have to give in to my sound reasoning.

"Gwen, no one is looking. Come on, I really want you to put your arm around me," she persisted.

"No, Linda."

"Yes, Gwen."

"No, I simply won't. I can't."

"Gwen, would you put your arm around me." She asked again, as if making a statement.

"Oh, all right." I gave in. We stuck our arms around each other and walked on in her victory. I had a mixed sense of intense uneasiness and triumph, with the bulk of the feeling on the uneasy side. Avoiding the glances of the passersby, we walked like two statues with moving legs, arms clasped around stony shoulders.

Coming close to Linda's apartment, I began to breathe a sigh of relief. *Well, I did it, and I'm glad it's almost over,* I thought. Just as a sense of accomplishment was beginning to set in, Linda stopped short on the sidewalk. *She's probably going to congratulate me,* I thought, a little self-satisfied.

She looked into my face and said, "Would you kiss me?"

"You're joking. Is this a test?" I replied incredulously. "Here? Now? No, that does it. That takes it. No. Right here? You're crazy! You want me to kiss you right here?"

"Well, you want to make love to me, don't you?" she asked with a mischievous expression.

"Yes, but not on the street!"

She stared without moving or changing expression.

"You're too fucking much," I said, laughing, my frustration bubbling to a climax. I put my arms around her and kissed her solidly on the lips.

"Happy now?" I questioned.

"Yes." She smiled. "Let's get going, it's damn cold out here."

Entering Linda's small three-room apartment, I noticed immediately how personal a space it was. The things on the walls, the books, records, plants, furniture, reeked of her feelings, thoughts, and values. I appreciated this aspect of her. In comparing it to my own place, I was horrified to realize that mine was really more early motel room than I had previously acknowledged to myself.

We shed our jackets, hats, gloves, and boots, and Linda said, "I'll make us some tea."

"Herbal tea, by any chance?" I ventured.

"Well, I do have the hard stuff, too."

"No, herbal's fine," I laughed.

While the water was warming, Linda put on some eerie sort of spiritual music and lit the candles in her bedroom. I sat on the makeshift couch, taking in the essence of the place.

When the tea was made, she said, moving toward the bedroom, cups in hand, "Come on, let's go in here."

She had a king-sized foam mattress supported by some crates and covered with a cotton Indian-design bedspread. We sat cross-legged on the bed and sipped our tea.

Candlelight was very becoming to Linda's handsome face. Without her glasses, she was incredibly soft-looking, her blue eyes remarkably beautiful. Her brown lashes were long and swept over her eyes when she blinked. Even though I had always thought her particularly attractive, I was taken by the radiance she emanated at that moment. She seemed a little shy and looked down a lot as we talked. Then, as if something had grabbed her, she looked up at me and stared deeply. I squirmed uneasily but felt compelled to look back.

She put our cups down and ran one hand lightly through my hair, pushing it off my forehead. Then she took the other hand and, with both, lightly caressed my face, stopping at times to cradle it in her palms.

Within this atmosphere of her beauty and tenderness, I felt myself turned on. I took one of her hands, brought it to my mouth, and kissed the palm. She pulled herself closer, removed her hand from my mouth, and, again holding my face, kissed me with moist, parted lips, tenderly, lightly. My lips tingled. Then she kissed my closed eyes, my forehead, cheeks, neck, breasts. She stopped my hands, moved close, and drew my arms around her. She wrapped her arms around my back and held me, not tightly, but with conviction.

We lay down together on the bed and held each other this way for a long time. The fresh-air smell of her hair and body penetrated my nostrils. I felt almost as if I were going in and out of consciousness, as if I might sink into her. I buried my head in her neck. We began to rock together, barely, slowly. I felt an awakening in my body. She began to massage my back and ass with her hands, gently. Periodically she would hold them still and pull me to her tightly. Then she pushed me away from her and started to unbutton my shirt, exposing my breasts. She unbuckled the belt, yanked the snap on my jeans, and pulled them down as I wiggled out. I moved my hands under her sweater and lightly ran them over her breasts. She moaned quietly and closed her eyes. I pulled the sweater over her head, then removed her jeans as she had mine. We embraced again and resumed our rocking.

I slipped my leg in between hers and maneuvered myself down, placing my jutting hip bone against her groin. Warm, wet liquid bathed my bone. We continued rocking more and more dramatically. I kissed her breasts and sucked the nipples and the skin surrounding them. She began to moan louder and in rhythm with our rocking. Her cunt began to grind hard against my slippery bone. She ran her spread labia over and over my protuberance, smoothly stroking herself. She grasped tightly, pulling and releasing my lower back. My own mushy clit ground into her thigh. I rolled over on top of her and continued dragging my come-smeared bone against her. My other leg straddled hers. Her pelvis rose against me, the movement of her leg stimulating me more. Grunting, I pushed myself against her harder. I began moving in a circular motion, alternately rubbing her and myself.

She began murmuring a progression of "oh's," stretching them out. She forcefully pulled my butt to her. She lifted her free leg and slung it over my back. We ground and slid over each other furiously. She rode my bone, pulling away slightly, then mashing herself into it. Her murmurs became deeper and louder. Then she pulled me violently to her and squeezed me between her legs. Her muscles contracted and I felt her burst, a stream of bubbling passion pouring over me. At that moment, my own lower belly, smothered in her legs, went into spasm. I screamed out in throbbing ecstasy, my body going rigid, our mutually popping pelvises bouncing, humping together. In constant motion, our movements slowed again; entangled, rocking softly, easily, small shots of pleasure continued to rise in us.

≈15

E arly the next morning I got up to leave Linda and go back to my apartment to change for work. She murmured as I threw on my clothes, "You're leaving?"

"Yeah, I've got to get going."

"Okay, I'll see you next Tuesday."

"Right," I muttered, looking down at her peaceful face. I bent down to kiss her and nuzzled her hair.

"Gwen, that was really nice, last night, I mean."

"Yeah, it was," I responded. I made a conscious effort to push down the warm, mushy feelings that were welling up in me. "See ya Tuesday, gorgeous."

"Gorgeous?" she said, inflamed. I exited quickly, chuckling at how easy it was to get her goat. Hustling down the street, a fleeting thought passed through me: Could I fall in love with Linda?

Linda and I sailed through the last two group sessions. The group members had built a solid rapport and were percolating along almost by themselves. Linda and I felt we could relax more, and we enjoyed the women immensely. People had made friends with one another and were talking about getting together socially. One of the women announced that she and her lover were planning a large party and invited us all. Separating was hard for us, and we all expressed our intentions to go to the party, to put off our inevitable parting. I knew it was going to be particularly hard for me not to see Linda on a regular basis. Who would I argue with now? But I knew I must not fall in love. Her resolve to stay free, although maybe somewhat weakened, was intact, and I couldn't afford another relationship I wasn't ready for.

The following Saturday evening I arrived at the party site on Fifteenth Street. Going up in the elevator, I wondered how our host was going to accommodate the number of people she had invited. When the doors opened, I got my answer. The elevator opened right into the apartment.

Coming off the elevator, I was initially a little disoriented. My host glided over and grabbed my arm, saying as she pulled me along, "Hi, Gwen, I'm so glad you came. Let me show you around so you can get your bearings; then I'll introduce you to people." She explained on the tour that she had gotten a really good deal on this loft space a few years earlier, and that she owned the entire floor. The apartment was like a ranch-style house, vast and complete.

In the huge living room I was struck by an awesome crowd of people. There appeared to be hundreds of gay men and lesbians, all dressed to the hilt. A long table was packed with food. There was also a band and, of course, a couple of bars. I immediately went for one, slugged down some confidence, then searched around the room for a familiar face for comfort.

I found one. A woman I had seen occasionally at the center was sitting in a corner with some other women. I ambled over and made myself at home. After a few social niceties and introductions, I sat down with the group and began to inspect the crowd more thoroughly. I searched for Linda but after a while resigned myself to the fact that she probably wasn't coming. I settled in with the flow.

The evening took off. I began flitting from group to group, finding acquaintances and meeting new ones. We danced and drank and snorted and smoked. We boogied and ripped and flew.

Near exhaustion at one point, I fled from the dance floor for a rest period. As my consciousness settled into a haze, I noticed an extraordinary wild creature flying around the dance floor. She was laughing gleefully, completely involved in her surroundings and taken by the abandonment of the moment. I couldn't take my eyes off her. She was adorable, with long auburn hair and a luscious petite but full frame. Eventually noticing my stare, she danced her way over to me and, smiling, outstretched her hands to me. I let out a hoot as she pulled me to my feet and onto the dance floor.

We danced together and with others and back together again. Amidst the loud music and noisy crowd I managed to get her name and her relationship with the host. But mostly we just smiled, laughed, and danced. I loved her lightness, her youthful spirit. She couldn't have been older than twenty-two.

Wearing out again, and for other reasons, I must admit, I began to hope for a slow dance. There hadn't been one all evening, but I knew they'd have to wind down eventually. At last the band leader announced a change of mood amidst a clamor of cheers and boos. I looked at my partner and said, "Phew. Good." She smiled back as if to say she could still go on but this was okay too.

Dancing slow with Stacy was a wonderful experience. She melted into me. Her body was like a magnet against mine. We swooned around the dance floor, totally relaxed in each other's arms. She adeptly used her limbs to put tension in the right places. She massaged my back and ass with her hand and edged her thigh in between my legs. We danced and danced, one dance after the other, changing our position not at all, but pressed together tighter and tighter. Her breasts squished into my rib cage as we slithered to the sweet romantic music. With my eyes closed, I had the sense that we were totally alone, almost forgetting about those around us. Desire began to overtake me as my crotch quivered. I wanted to make love to this woman immediately, but at the same time knew I would really want to draw this one out to the last drop. As Stacy and I floated in our symbiotic ballet, she whispered, "Would you like to go to my place?"

Breaking out of my trance, I said, "Sure!"

We slipped off the floor, at last found our coats, and without proper adieus, whisked ourselves out onto the street. We grabbed a cab and within a few minutes found ourselves in her lower East Side studio.

Once inside, as if we had been pent up for years, we plunged into each other. Still standing by the door, kissing with fervor, I began fumbling with Stacy's slacks, pulling them partway down, and moving my hand into her warm fur. She gasped suddenly when my fingers swept over her. She shook her slacks and underpants to the floor, and I immediately fell to my knees and began sucking her. She spread her legs wide, and I pursued her even more, licking and sucking as if starved. She pressed her hands down on my shoulders to raise herself up. Her breath came hard. With a shaky voice she croaked, "Let's lie down."

Peeling off the rest of her clothes and mine, we jumped onto the bed, embracing each other. While she tongued my ear, she said low, "Gwen, I want you to do something for me."

"Anything," I said, with a breathy voice.

She rolled away, reached into a drawer beside her bed, and pulled out four leather straps. Holding them in front of me, she said, "I want you to tie me."

"Tie you?" I asked stupidly.

"Yeah, you know, to the bed," she responded, with both a twinkle and great seriousness in her eyes.

"Oh," I said. Not wishing to delay things with a conversation, I decided, *Fuck it, I'll think about it later.* I took the straps and tied her wrists to the headboard and her ankles to the sides of the bed at the bottom.

Instinct took over. I lay on top of her and pressed my body hard on hers, grinding bone on bone and mashing her breasts. I kissed her hard on the mouth, plunging my tongue inside until I thought I would touch the back of her throat. She ground back against me and wiggled and rotated her torso against mine. The force of our movements excited me immediately, and my knob began to twitch with sensation. I wanted her breasts. Moving down, I took the hard, erect, pale nipples into my mouth.

She said, "Hard, do it hard." I sucked with force, taking as much as I could hold and drawing it up.

"Bite it," she murmured.

I bit gently, teasingly.

"Harder, bite harder."

I bit hard on the area around the nipple, squeezing it inside my mouth, flicking it with my tongue. Her bosom swelled as she fought to shove it toward me.

Panting, she said, "Bite the nipple."

Taking the nipple between my teeth, I bit it gently at first, then harder. She opened her mouth full and huffed. Gasping, she said, "Yes, yes, oh yes." Her chest arched.

Moving my hand to her mouth, I stuck in my fingers. She sucked and bit them. With my other hand I reached down and pushed against her mound. She thrust herself up, her legs pulling against the straps. I shoved my fingers into her hole, pushing two, then three, into the soft tissue. Now yanking on the straps above, she scraped herself over my fingers as if to swallow my arm.

"Harder, oh harder," she gurgled. "In the drawer."

Taking my hand from her mouth, I pulled open her bedside drawer. Inside lay a large, pink, bumpy dildo. I took the tickler out and replaced my fingers with it. As it entered her, she yelled out and pulled violently on the straps above, pushing her pelvis down on the dildo with all her might. Throwing my legs over on one of hers, I spread myself over her. I began ramming the tickler into her, still crushing her nipples between my teeth. Her whole body fought against the straps, her arms pulling down and legs pulling up. Her torso jerked against the twisting, thumping rubber. My own cunt throbbed as I smeared it over her leg. I dove and shoved as I ground myself into her taut and struggling body.

She howled, "Harder, harder, oh God, oh yes."

Suddenly she let out a blood-curdling scream. Her body jolted frantically against the restraints. She shook violently, thrashing against the dildo. She yanked and pulled until I thought she'd break out of her confinement.

Slowing down, I eased the dildo back and forth gently in her canal. As she came to rest, her legs and belly twitched and trembled. She moaned softly, her mouth open and eyes closed, as if unconscious. I laid my head against her purple breast and felt numb all over.

ॐ16

It had been quite a while since I had seen Sarah for any length of time. Since Linda and I had started the group, Sarah and I had just sort of passed each other in the night, breezing by with a quick smile and hug. I didn't like that, and now that the group was over, I gleefully anticipated my reward: Sarah's attention and gratitude. I also had lots to fill her in on since we had last talked. I knew she would be amazed that Linda and I had gotten together and wondered how she would respond. How would she feel about her colleague and I making it? Would I perceive that same sort of funny sadness from her I had experienced when I had been with Fran?

And I wanted to talk with her about my brief S&M experience. I wanted to air my feelings about it and find out where she stood.

We planned to meet for dinner in a quaint restaurant, one of the oldest in the Village, near her apartment. I was early, as I always was for my appointments with Sarah. Sitting in this pleasant atmosphere, I remarked to myself how appropriate it was to be meeting her here. It was like her. It was small and freshly painted, with a comfortable, bright, and simple but tasteful ambience. It was old; under the neat, crisp exterior lay an old, wise room.

My anxiety level was rising again. When it got to the point that I started jiggling my legs and tapping my fingers, Sarah bustled in as if from out of nowhere.

"Hi, Gwen," she beamed.

"Hi, Sarah," I said, mimicking her enthusiasm. She laughed and dropped into a chair. "It's been so long since we've gotten together," I continued.

"I know, too long," she agreed. "But we're here now. I'm so happy to see you. I've heard so many good things about the group; it was a real success. I knew you'd be good at it," she congratulated me. "When are you going to do another one?"

I got my reward. "Wait a minute!" I said, trying to control my show of satisfaction. "Maybe we'll do another one, but not right away."

"Yeah, you deserve a break. Not for too long, though," she said, pouting for a second, then regaining her positive posture.

I unraveled some of the details of the group and ended with the story of Leadership Leads to Love. She listened intently, a slight frown edging her face.

"I would never have thought that you two would get together," she said seriously. Then, flippantly, "You're the most unlikely pair." She paused. "Maybe, come to think of it, you two would be good for each other, if you survived."

I smiled and had to agree, although deep down I felt a bit of that nudging longing I had experienced and been fighting off since my encounter with Linda.

"Now don't go jumping to conclusions. This was strictly casual and probably will never happen again," I admonished both her and myself.

When I began to relate my experience at the party and after, Sarah started to play with her straw, sliding the wrapper down it, crushing the paper together to form a snake, then putting drops of water on it, making it slowly crawl open. It was as if The Answer would be exposed when the paper stretched out again.

"What do you think of S&M?" I asked. "To be perfectly frank," I admitted, "I was a little shook up, but it turned me on, too."

"Well," she said, looking down as if reading her answer from the wet glob of paper, "I don't really understand it, except maybe from the perspective of a power thing. You know, we participate in verbal and emotional S&M all the time. In a way, it's sort of an acting out physically of what we all do on an emotional level. I think I'd have to explore it more before I could form an opinion. But I'm not going to — explore it, I mean," she said, giggling.

I thought, feeling more at ease, *Neither am I.*

Through the rest of the dinner we gabbed, mostly light-heartedly. Sarah filled me in on what she had been doing, and her latest thoughts on her vocation, where she thought she was going or wasn't going. As usual, during dessert, as I dove into my sweet binge, the child came out of Sarah. She always ordered something smaller than I, and then, having devoured it, would start on what I couldn't finish. While she picked, she threw out our evening plan.

"Gwen, there's a group I've been going to lately. It's really good. It's a place where people get together and talk about what stops them from really being what they want to be. They claim that by continually putting out and hearing others put out what sort of self-destructive things they do in their lives, it gets better. And, you know, I think they're right. Since I've been going, I feel like it might be possible for me to rise above negative impulses in a way, to come out from under. It's hard to explain, but I want you to see it. Will you come with me tonight?"

Something she said struck me. I'd been trying to figure out what was wrong with me. No matter where I went, I seemed to take myself with me. I couldn't really escape. When my life wasn't filled with some sort of external jumble, there seemed to be only emptiness left. Although a little disappointed that I wasn't going to be spending the evening exclusively with Sarah, I said, "Okay, let's go."

We arrived at a church basement hall. Men and women were packed together, some even standing. A woman was speaking. Surveying the crowd, I ascertained this to be a mixed group of gay and straight. After the speaker, who was extremely funny and candid, people began to talk one at a time. They seemed brutally honest about their shortcomings and the personal problems in their lives. I was astonished at the show of pain and joy. They talked of how they had changed previous disasters into new triumphs, how little by little they were better able to make correct behavioral choices. And, most importantly, how they were finding a person in themselves amidst all the rubble.

Sarah and I would glance sideways at each other and smile when someone said something we knew particularly applied to us individually. It seemed to me that people were talking about my life. I felt like a person dying of thirst being given a sip of water. By the end of the meeting I knew that in small continuous doses, I had to have more.

When the meeting was over, Sarah introduced me to some people she had met. They were friendly and welcoming. One woman in particular struck me. She approached me cautiously, almost self-consciously, but I was surprised, when she spoke, to see her air of shyness give way to confidence and authority. She was attractive — small, wonderfully curved, with a gorgeous head of short blonde curls. Her pug nose and slightly crooked teeth lent her a boyish quality. She had a sort of Peter Pan essence, a look of never-ending youth.

Hearing someone call her Spike, I questioned her nickname. She told me with pleasure that before coming to the group, her nickname had been Mouse. All that was changed now.

Well, she admitted, at least the name and some of that was changed now. I could definitely see the Spike in her.

❧17

I started to go several times a week to the group. Sometimes Sarah was there too. I got to know the other people and enjoyed talking and listening to them. It was hard for me to talk in the group, but I discovered when I did that some of the power seemed to come out of whatever was bothering me. The most astonishing thing was that I went there not for Sarah or because she might be there. Although I enjoyed the others, I wasn't even going to be social. I went for myself. I had suddenly found a minuscule fiber inside that was me, and I was nurturing it. I tried to stay away from sexual encounters so as to concentrate on my new self-awareness. But every now and then, particularly when I spent time with Spike, I was made aware that the old me was alive and well. I took to her cute boy-girl essence. And she seemed to love to be touched, a quality I found to be a major turn-on.

One night after a meeting, I approached Spike and asked if she'd like to go out for something to eat. She said, "Oh, Gwen, I would like to, but I'm so exhausted and grungy. I've been in Washington all day."

"Okay," I said, feeling slightly rejected. "Maybe some other time."

"No," she said firmly, suddenly changing her mind. "Let's go tonight. But let's stop at my apartment first so I can jump in the tub and change my clothes."

"It's a deal," I said, my self-confidence restored.

As we rode in the cab to her place, Spike was quiet. I jabbered my enthusiasm about the group and how I felt I was growing from it. I explained that I was feeling more filled, more complete than I had in years. She listened, smiling and nodding and occasionally adding her own experience and changes.

"It's good to know that you don't have to be driven by the same repeated patterns of behavior generated by obsessions and insecurities," she said.

"Or grandiose delusions," I added. Searching her face for a clue of what she was feeling about us being together, I noticed she did in fact look very tired. Ah, a hard-working woman, I thought. I resigned myself to the fact that dinner was probably all that would be on the agenda for tonight.

Spike had a nice, rather small, cozy apartment that she seemed to make the best of, as so many of us do. She had utilized her space well and brightened it to the fullest possible extent.

Throwing off her coat and grabbing mine, she said, "Help yourself to anything you want. I'll just be a few minutes." She whisked off into the bathroom.

I sat down, lit a cigarette, and began thumbing through the latest edition of *Womanews*. I heard water running and saw the shadowed figure of Spike removing her clothes. Then the whoosh of water stopped, and I could hear her plunk herself in with a loud sigh. *She's leaving the door open*, I thought. *An invitation? Shit no*, I reprimanded myself. *She probably wants to be able to talk to me while bathing.* Sure enough, she began calling out little blurbs about her job, her day, and various trivialities. Making small comments back, I found myself getting increasingly agitated. I had this driving impulse to see her lying in the tub.

"Gwen, you haven't said much about your job," she yelled. "It must be very interesting."

At that point I slinked into the bathroom and, standing by the tub, looked down at her soapy, slippery, smooth skin bobbing in the water. She had a head full of shampoo and her eyes were closed from the soap dripping down her face.

"Gwen, is your job interesting?" she repeated louder.

"Very interesting," I said in low, drawn-out tones.

She jumped, washed the soap from her eyes, and stared at me, first with fear, then with amusement.

In silence, I removed my clothes slowly, then slipped into the tub. As she sat up, I placed myself in behind her with my legs on either side of her. We sank down, and I pulled her back against my chest and stomach. My hands glossed over her chest, down her belly, and around her thighs, sliding over her lubricated curves. She moved her back against my chest and pushed the small of her back into my submerged crotch.

I took the soap and lathered her all over. I massaged the suds around her breasts, under her arms, along her thighs, and, reaching forward, met her bent legs jutting out of the water. She jumped slightly when my hands skimmed her knees. Taking the cue, I ran my fingers around the knobby part of her knees. She giggled and growled. Circling her kneecap, I reached under and tickled behind her knees. She quivered and yelped, goose bumps forming on her skin. As I continued to play, she lifted her feet out of the water and put

– 87 –

them up on the lower edge of the tub. I reached farther and incorporated the upper part of her calf, running my fingers around and up and over behind her knees. She began to shove herself against my front with more force, wiggling into me, rotating her upper buttocks.

The foamy water surged around us, swishing and gulping. I brought my hands up to her bobbing breasts and floated around them, lifting and dropping. I brushed her nipples with my palms again and again. She brought her feet back into the tub and pushed herself with force against me. I moved my hands up to her neck and caressed the nape, around to her collarbone and along the edge of it. I brushed her hair from her forehead and ran my fingers through her hair and back down to her ears. With one hand I rotated a finger in one canal, licking the other with my tongue. I plunged my tongue into the hole and lapped around her upper ear. She pressed her head toward my tongue, moaning softly. I took her earlobe into my mouth and sucked it, alternating this with tongue darts into the opening.

Leaving her ear, I tongued behind and below it, tasting soap as I kissed where hairline meets skin. She hung her head down and continued to moan.

Suddenly she pulled forward and unplugged the tub. Turning her body around, she knelt in between my legs and kissed my lips, running her tongue lightly around the inner edge of them. I held her head forward, clasping her wet curls in my palms. As the water sank away, she reached over and plugged something over the spout. She turned on the faucet, then took the shower massager and began washing suds off my languid torso. The water pulsed over me, sweeping my neck and breasts and belly button. She began to rinse my legs and inner thighs. She switched the spray to pummel and the water began shooting out in forceful bursts. She zeroed in on my lathered cunt. My clit awakened from its soapy slumber and jabs of pleasure ran down my legs. The teasing water forced me down into the tub. I pulled at her hands, begging for more.

Playing on my urgency, Spike moved the spray away from me and quickly rinsed herself off. With a towel, she hurriedly dried both of us. We emerged from the tub, half carrying each other to the bed.

Laying me down on my back, Spike fell on top of me. We mashed together, thrusting tongues in and out of each other's mouths. I grasped and pulled her buttocks into me. She bumped her jutting pubic bone against my enraged clitoris, forcing my legs to spread around hers. She mashed and released, mashed and released.

"More, faster," I yelled in agony, shots of pleasure bringing me so close but keeping me on the edge.

Then she raised herself up and pulled my body over so I lay on my stomach, arms stretched out to the side. She rotated her hands around my butt and up my back, barely scraping my skin. I jumped and shuddered each time she brought her nails down my spine to my crevice.

Spreading my legs further, she slipped her fingers inside my melting hole. She slid them in and out, pressing lightly on that sensitive spot inside. I grunted, red with heat. Then, taking both hands, she spread my buttocks wide open. She encircled my anus with her tongue, plunging it in and around. The wildly pleasurable sensation caused my back and stomach to quiver and jump uncontrollably. Masterfully keeping me spread with one hand, she moved the other underneath and stroked my clit with her first two fingers, sticking her thumb into me, sliding her fingers over my clit. My lower half raged with excitement. I howled and ground into the bed, holding the sides with outstretched arms.

Driving me to the brink again, she slowed her movements. In a cry of ultimate frustration, I screamed, "Please, do it! Don't stop; do it!"

Shoving her stiff tongue inside me, she ran her fingers with a frenzy over my throbbing cunt, pushing me over the threshold into a deep abyss, my body parts flying away from each other, then contracting again. A powerful force of incredible pleasure jolted up through my arms and down my legs. I cried out as the sensation burst forth again and again.

Spike laid herself on top of my exhausted, shaking body, still face down on the bed. I felt her breathe heavily in my ear as she nuzzled me. Our chests heaved together, mutually expanding and contracting. After a few moments she began to sway gently from side to side, spreading her legs on each side of my ass. Her soft murmurs blown into my ear sent chills down my spine. Continuing to rotate her crotch into my meaty cheeks, she brought her fingers up to and into my mouth. I sucked and drooled on them as she played with my lips and teeth.

Taking the initiative, I turned over, moving Spike onto her side. Sliding down with my head at the end of the bed, I lifted up her leg and moved myself in, crotch to crotch, scissoring our bodies together. We began to move genital against genital. The wetness flowed out of us as we smeared ourselves over each other. My own passion began to rise up again as our hot, soaking vulvas crawled over each other.

Spike began to breathe heavily and loudly, interjecting whimpering noises. I ran my hands down her legs and lower belly, kneading her flesh, pulling her toward me as we gyrated. Liquid glistened on our inner thighs. A pungent sweet-sour smell of burning desire emanated from us, penetrating my nostrils into my brain. We moved as one, rubbing and pushing, clit against clit. Spike began to pant and grunt, her face contorted. Moving more violently against me, her legs began to stiffen and tremble. I took my cue and began moving harder and faster against her. With the increased motion, Spike began to howl. We rolled over and over each other, shoving our pelvises together, the slime of our passion mingled and dripping. I clamped my legs hard, clasping her between them as if to shake her body between two large jaws.

Gripping my legs with her hands as if trying to hold them still, Spike went suddenly rigid. She gasped, then exploded. A force seemed to emanate from her thighs and, like a wave, crashed through her torso, her belly jumping, bosom swelling. She seized and jerked, her muscles going off independently of one another, then coming together again. Her whole body heaved, shuddered and sank. She lay still, heavy, fleeting twitches running through her.

❧ 18

O
ne warm June evening Sarah and I sat on the stoop of her apartment in the Village, slurping on ice cream cones. We lazily relaxed, watched the passersby, soaked up the warm evening air, and engrossed ourselves in the sweet sticky substance in our hands. Lapping up drips as they ran down the sides of the cones, we talked and laughed about the people, places, and things in our lives.

"You know, Sarah, I think the past year, since just before I met you up until now, has been both the best and the hardest year of my life. Nothing compares to the excitement of coming out in New York, but nothing compares to the scariness of it either. I feel like I'm just coming to terms with myself, now, a little. I have a sense of what it is that's been missing. I know now that what's been missing is me. But even though I know this, it's quite another thing to do something about it. It seems like I get going on a roll, you know, that I begin to act out of an integration of mind, body, and spirit, then I slide back into wanting to fill up my life with a lot of chaos, lots of things that provide a smoke screen so that I don't have to deal with that empty, boring, meaningless person somewhere deep down I fear I am. But during these times of integration — I guess you could call it centeredness or wholeness — I certainly don't feel boring or meaningless. I just don't know why I can't keep it up. I mean, why is it all so up and down?"

Sarah nodded slowly and intermittently bobbed her head emphatically as though she could identify strongly.

"It's the same way for me," she said. "I think it's fear. Sometimes I get scared of that person inside me. Like I don't have any idea who she is or what she's capable of. You know, Gwen, I almost think I'm afraid that if I get to know myself, get to feeling that sort of integration you were talking about, I might be so successful I wouldn't be able to stand it. Maybe I'd die or something. Sometimes I think it's easier to cope with the feelings of pain from known sources, like a fucked-up relationship, than the overwhelming joy I can experience when I clear the junk out of my life. I know how to handle the pain much better than the joy; I've had more practice. I heard someone say recently that we could all have lives filled with joy if we really wanted it. We seem to prevent it from happening a lot of times."

"Yeah, but what about death and loss and suffering and all that stuff? You can't feel joy all the time," I countered.

It suddenly occurred to me that I spent a lot of time preparing myself for destruction. "You know what?" I mused aloud. "I think much of what I do is preparation, like practice for the pain. It's like I'm constantly testing myself to see if I can endure it."

"And joy is not good practice for pain?" she asked.

"Something like that," I mused.

"I think one of the pitfalls is that we believe it has to be all or nothing. You know, if I feel joy today, I'd better make sure it lasts forever. Or if I feel pain today, I think it will last forever for sure. It's like the basic concept we have of heaven and hell, all good or all bad. You know, what's always fascinated me is the belief certain religious people have that at some point in the future, God will take up all the good people to heaven all at once. I can see it now. The *Post* reads: 'Mother swooped to heaven while giving birth.'"

I laughed.

"Even what it's called, 'the rapture,' seems to imply total joy," Sarah continued. "It's like this fantasy that humankind has that at some point all those deserving will be taken quickly and painlessly to a place of bliss."

"I know!" I said. "Maybe all the men will be taken and leave the earth finally to us."

"Then where is heaven?" she asked mischievously. "Maybe ... maybe, the idea should be more that the rapture is now," she pursued. "I mean that it's in all of us. That we could be lifted at any time out of our misery if we just want to be badly enough."

"You mean, rise above our circumstances, so to speak?" I asked, a little sarcastically.

"Not exactly." She spoke slowly, staring down at her wiggling toes with a slight smile. "More like meeting our circumstances as a whole person: a person in touch with the physical, emotional, intellectual, and spiritual in herself. Not perceived as parts, but each experienced as a whole and operating together. To experience ourselves fully. We'd be more able to handle the pain of failing that way. It wouldn't be so scary. Somehow I think we'd be able to absorb that we are loved for ourselves, for being, not for what we do."

"You mean something like, maybe if I could recognize all those things that I see in you in myself, I would feel as good by myself as I do when I'm with you?" I asked, half jokingly.

"Uh, something like that," she responded, with a patient glance.

"Okay, I'm an incorrigible pain in the ass," I admitted. "But it's all a process, right? I guess I don't really think any more that if you'd marry me, I'd be happy ever after. But we could give it a try!"

She giggled and blushed. "It's real hard to give up the idea that all your happiness can come from someone else," she said with a smile, tipping her head to one side. "Come on, let's go for a walk."

We stretched ourselves with effort off the stoop. With arms flung around each other, we strolled. I could see a patch of glimmering river between the buildings ahead, reflecting the sun going down in New Jersey.

This is my story, this is my song.

Late Spring

ᔰ*19*

I awoke with a start from my deep, drugged sleep. My head ached and my mouth was very dry. My eyes scanned the familiar institutional gray-white walls and floor. The window was open slightly and I felt damp, cool air on my face.

Something moved abruptly next to me. I looked toward the movement and remembered. Yeah, it was all coming back to me now as I gazed into the sleeping face of my latest friend, Pat. Her dark, long hair lay straggly, winding its way around the pillow. I felt a shot of embarrassment and pleasure at the same time, as my memory gave me away.

God, my mouth was dry. I got up to go to the bathroom — some Tylenol and cold water to my rescue. As I stood watching my swollen eyes in the mirror while brushing my teeth, I heard another movement from the bed. Glancing over, I noticed how smoothly the sheet clung to my friend's body, betraying every curve and crevice. *I have to get some silk sheets*, I thought, briefly.

As I continued to gaze at her delicate peaceful presence, I thought, *It sure doesn't look like there's anything wrong*. My mind flashed back to a conversation we had had the night before, sitting at the bar where we'd met. We had already established that we were mutually attracted. I was merely waiting for the right moment for one of us to suggest going home together.

We chatted, sipped our drinks, and watched the clamor of activity around us. I was getting more excited as time passed, and my mind raced with images of making love with this tall, slim, dark-haired woman with the sweet smile and large brown eyes. I guessed her to be about twenty-five.

Then my friend began a conversation, almost a confession of sorts, that sent me whirling into a frenzy of indecision.

"Gwen, there's something I have to discuss with you," she said, with a seriousness that effectively broke through the lightness of the moment. I began to try to joke, to break the tension, but was stopped in my tracks by the look on her face.

"What, Pat? What is it?" I said, now genuinely concerned.

She continued, "I haven't been out that long — maybe about a year or so. Before coming out I wasn't sure of my sexuality. Most of my sexual experiences have been with men."

"Yeah, so, that's okay," I interrupted. "Everybody comes out in their own way. Do you think I'm going to condemn you for sleeping with men? Most of us have slept with men at some point in our lives, I think." I wondered, *God, does she think this is some big deal?*

As if in answer to my question, Pat continued her story. "It's not the fact that I've slept with men that I need to discuss. It's that, well, as a result of it, I recently found out that I'm HIV-positive." She stopped talking for a moment.

I didn't know what to say, think, or do. I sat, trying to let the information sink into my brain and sort itself out. Then Pat helped me out.

"You see, it doesn't mean we can't make love tonight. There are ways that we can do it safely. I wouldn't be putting you in any danger, as long as we stick to the methods that I've learned. But I want you to know, if this makes you uncomfortable or frightened, I understand."

"You know, Pat," I said when I got my thoughts together, "I never even think about AIDS when I make love with women. I mean, it never occurs to me to worry about it. This blows my mind a little. What a bummer for you," I said with sudden empathy. "Have you been sick at all?"

"No," she said with some relief in her voice. "Luckily I've felt very well. I don't feel like there's anything wrong. But it frightens me sometimes to the point where I don't think I can bear it," she confessed. "There are support groups and that's helped a lot. Also, there are a lot of people really fighting to get some action in terms of research and treatments and just plain taking care of people who are sick. And in a way, knowing that I'm HIV-positive has kind of changed the quality of my life — in a good way, I mean. I don't waste time as much anymore. Everything is a little more precious. I don't get bogged down with junk worries like so many people do. And I really appreciate my health — I don't take it for granted."

As Pat talked I found myself a little afraid but also intrigued. She was inspiring. I found myself wanting to make love with her more than ever. But I needed a little more reassurance.

"Are you certain that we can make love safely?" I asked, hoping for the right answer.

"Yes," she said emphatically. "I have all the stuff we might need. And you don't have to do anything that makes you uncomfortable. Basically, we have to be careful about body fluids and blood."

"Can I kiss you?" I asked, thinking of saliva as a fluid.

"Yes," she said, nodding, "all indications are that the virus doesn't hang out much in the mouth. But again, do it only if you're comfortable with it."

I leaned over toward her and kissed her lightly on the lips. "Feels pretty comfortable," I said, smiling. She laughed. "Come on, let's go to my place and see what magic tricks you have," I said, grabbing her hand. I hoped that my air of gaiety would hide the ambivalence I was feeling. We slid off the stools and made our way into the cool night.

My reverie was broken and I was brought swiftly back to the present when the still, peaceful body that I was staring at spoke. "Gwen, I feel awful," it said.

"I'll bring you some hangover remedies in one second," the nurse in me responded. I went over and sat on the edge of the bed, medicine and water in hand.

"Here, sit up so you don't choke," I instructed.

"I wish I would," she said with a short laugh. Her perfect white teeth aided her beautiful smile. I remembered immediately what had first attracted me to this woman. My daze was clearing and keen hot sensations were coming through.

"What time is it?" Pat asked, as she fell back flat onto the bed.

"Oh, it's really early," I lied. "It's Saturday anyway, who cares what time it is?" She smiled and closed her eyes. Her face relaxed and I thought she was falling back to sleep.

My eyes were drawn to the sheet again. Slowly I moved my hand over the sheet where the curves were, the material offering no resistance to my stroke. I glanced, for a moment, at the latex gloves lying on the bedside table. I dismissed them — if I needed them later, I'd put them on. I rode my hand over one breast, then the other, my palm massaging the nipples. Then slowly I moved my hand down her midline, stopping at her tummy. I pressed and circled it from just the edge of her pubic bone to her ribs.

Her breathing became heavier and her legs moved slightly farther apart. I continued my journey downward, sliding my hand over the crevice in between her legs. Back and forth I ran my fingers, finding a warm place under the sheet. Her legs spread farther now and her body began rocking in rhythm with my back-and-forth movements.

I briefly left this burning place and ran my hand quickly over her inner thigh, then back all the way up to her breasts. Now I engaged my other hand, circling her breasts, palming the nipples. Then with both hands I caressed her whole body, dipping frequently into that crevice.

Her movements became more and more pronounced, and I felt myself rocking to her rhythm. My face felt flushed and small beads of sweat were forming on me. With sudden abandonment, I quickly edged my body on top of hers over the sheet. That same grace of movement the sheet provided for my hand did as well for my body, and I began sliding it smoothly in that circular motion over hers, breast to breast, pelvis to pelvis.

Just when I thought we were both about to burst under our movement, I stopped completely. Within seconds she stopped too. We lay still for what seemed like a long time. Then I kissed her parted lips softly, and starting at her mouth, my tongue began the journey my hand and body had taken.

My mouth dragged the sheet down as I sucked and kissed the skin of her neck, under her arms, her breasts. When my mouth reached her nipples her movements began again, accompanied by moans and sighs. I yanked the sheet off and slid my mouth down her body to the crevice.

There, in place from the night before, was a thin, soft layer of rubber held over her crotch by efficient-looking straps. The texture of the rubber was almost like skin. My tongue searched over the smooth film looking for that small spot of pleasure-giving tissue. Soon, my tongue felt what it was looking for. The stimulated spot felt harder than the rest of her. The discovery of it sent chills of excitement through me. She too became more animated. Her pelvis began to rise and fall, her upper thighs stiffened and relaxed. I licked her slowly, firmly, pausing at times to press my contracted tongue hard against her raging pulsating clitoris, now soaked in its own juices under the slippery cloak.

My lover's hands now grasped the sheets, squeezing so tightly as to make her knuckles white. Her moans became gasps as the rising sensations in her surged and billowed to completion. My own hands clung to her torso, squeezing it tightly in my own tension and abandonment.

Then her pelvis jerked and went rigid in the air. "Oh, God," she called out. Tiny tremors rippled her upper thighs. I felt her body trembling where I held to it. Slowly and with a great sigh she then floated her body back onto the bed. I laid my head on her stomach. In the stillness of our repose, I felt on my face the small jerks that emanated from her muscle in relaxation.

"Aren't you glad it's Saturday?" I asked finally. She giggled.

❧ 20

*T*he stone steps in front of the Gay and Lesbian Service Center felt a little cold as I sat on them in the early evening, waiting for my meeting with Sarah. She was always late, but I always excused her. This time she probably got hung up with someone after her group. Some needy person, who really just had a crush on her, had managed to grab her attention. And I knew I was a little jealous of that, although used to it.

As I waited I enjoyed the ambiance of the Village streets in the spring. The winter passes, and along with the first signs of warm weather come all these people — so many people. I always wondered where they came from, and where they went when it was cold. Anyway, it was one of the perks of living in New York — one was always entertained.

I always sat in anticipation when waiting for Sarah. But I was acutely aware of how much that feeling had diminished. My mind began to wander over the changes in the last year. I still wanted her to love me, and still knew I wouldn't kick her out of bed. But things had changed. As our friendship grew more important, the lust diminished. By now I was really sure about what Sarah wanted from our relationship. And as much as there were times, especially when she and her lover had broken up, that I wanted to run to her and present my case again, I knew very well that that was not what she needed from me.

She needed a real friend. More than anything, that was what she lacked. To most people, she was a counselor. She had few people she could be with on an equal plane. She had chosen me as one of those people. And I knew I was as important to her as any of those few in her life that she had loved a great deal. As time went on I grew satisfied with this as my role in her life. Any other feelings toward her were beginning to feel incestuous.

There was the side issue also of my relationship with Linda. I laughed when I caught myself thinking of Linda as a side issue. She, of course, was a main issue.

Linda and I had begun a relationship several months earlier. We were going hot and heavy just when Sarah was going through her breakup. The timing was shitty. But the reality was that timing or not, Sarah didn't want me as a lover, and Linda, this gorgeous, wonderful person, did. It was all working out rather nicely, actually, except for a few little quirks.

I thought when Linda and I finally made that big plunge to move in together that monogamy would fall into place. Well, it did for Linda, but not for me. As much as I convinced myself that the reason for keeping a room at the nurses' residence at the hospital was just in case things didn't work out, I knew way down deep the real reason I kept it. I really loved Linda and wanted to be with her, but I just couldn't commit myself to not being with other women sexually. I was quite sure I wasn't about to fall in love with anyone else. I really had the capacity to be in love with just one woman at a time. And that person was definitely Linda.

Suddenly Sarah stuck her head out the door and said brightly, "Hi. I'll be there in one minute. I just have to put up a few flyers. Oh," she paused, "do you want to help me?"

"Sure," I said, without energy.

As we hung the flyers Sarah told me enthusiastically about the event she was advertising. "I'm not going, but I think you'd love it," she said with ironic sincerity.

"Yeah, maybe I'll go," I said to appease her. "Come on, let's go, it's a great night!" I prodded.

"Isn't it a wonderful night," she exclaimed as we burst out the doors. "I'm so glad we could get together."

"Yeah," I said, realizing she hadn't heard me before. "Where do you want to go?" I asked.

"Um," she began to think out loud, "we could go for a walk or get some coffee or we could get ice cream and sit on my stoop. Oh, yeah, do you want to get some ice cream?" she asked hopefully.

"I have an idea — let's go to Stella's for a drink," I said with conviction.

"Okay, that'll be fun, I haven't been there in a long time," she said.

Stella's was a tiny lesbian bar about a block from the center. I liked its smallness and I liked Stella. Walking toward our destination, I noted the streets were even more crowded than before. Sarah just kept beaming — she loved warm weather.

We sat at a tiny table against the back wall at Stella's. The room was barren of people, just a few barflies hanging around. There was virtually no ambiance. It was just a dimly lit room where one could stop and get a few drinks and cruise a small but loyal crowd.

Sarah ordered a wine cooler and I, my usual, vodka martini. Sarah didn't drink much and I was soon ordering a second, while she had barely touched her wine. Any anxiety I might have had while waiting for Sarah soon drifted away and a feeling of well-being took over. *There's nothing like booze as a social lubricant*, I thought.

"So how is life in Brooklyn?" Sarah asked. Her face was filled with the anticipation of hearing all about my married life.

"Well," I started, "I'm not crazy about Brooklyn, but we do have a nice apartment. I wish you'd come over some time. We have a neat fireplace."

"Maybe I could come for dinner? I'd bring something," she suggested.

"That would be great," I agreed.

There was a hesitation in our conversation. I was trying to decide if I could talk to Sarah openly about my feelings and behavior. She seemed to be waiting for me to decide.

"You know it's been difficult for me to maintain total monogamy in my relationship," I began. "It's weird, because being in a relationship, especially with Linda, is really what I want. But it's like I'm afraid to put all of my eggs in one basket. You know, what if it doesn't last?"

"Tell me about it," Sarah said, half smiling.

I continued, "Linda and I are so different in so many ways, I don't know how we got together in the first place."

"I know," Sarah burst out. "It's really hard to see you two together. But it's really neat, too. I think you're good for her."

I sensed Sarah's bias.

"Don't be too hard on yourself. You're probably just scared," she advised. "Can you talk about this with Linda?"

"Hell, no!" I shouted.

A few people at the bar turned their heads toward us. More quietly, I admonished, "And don't you tell her. It would ruin everything." Sarah assured me my secrets were safe with her.

Through the evening we talked and shared our most intimate thoughts. I was becoming looser with mine as I drank. Sarah had such a nice trait of being totally nonjudgmental. She didn't even seem to notice that by the end of the evening I was loaded.

Sarah walked me to the subway entrance and gave me a big hug goodbye. It was so nice to know someone loved my jerky self, just as I was.

21

When I arrived home I was still drunk. On the way home, I thought of nothing else but having a wild sexual fling with Linda upon my arrival. She was in bed reading when I walked through the door.

"Hi, hon," I said.

"Hi, hon," she replied, offhandedly. I sat on the bed trying to clear my vision.

"You reek!" Linda snapped.

"Yeah, Sarah and I went to Stella's," I confessed.

"Oh, did you have a good talk?" she asked. Her voice had a ring of jealousy I didn't want to get into.

"Yeah, you know, the usual good time," I said casually.

I didn't want to talk, and I began to make moves to express what I did want to do. Linda shrugged me off.

"Gwen, you know I don't like to make love when you're drunk," she reminded me.

"Oh, come on, I'm not drunk. I just had a couple of drinks," I defended myself.

"Yes, you are drunk, and besides I'm in a different space than you are. You're all hyped up and I'm tired. I'm ready to go to sleep."

"Oh, God forbid I should disrupt your precious sleep," I yelled. "Fuck it." I jumped off the bed, yanked up my pillow and a blanket, and went off to the living room.

"Gwen," Linda called. "Come on, don't sleep in there. Gwen?"

"Leave me alone. I'm sleeping in here — that way I won't disturb you," I snapped, rubbing it in.

I lay down on the couch and instantly fell asleep.

I woke up in the middle of the night, my body aching from being in one stiff position for several hours. Immediately a rotten feeling of remorse set in. *I hate to fight,* I thought. *But she's such a bitch sometimes.*

I got up and made a cup of tea, lit a cigarette, and sat staring at the cold fireplace. There was a bitter chill in the air. I felt wide awake and knew I wouldn't be able to fall back to sleep. I decided to make a fire, so I'd have something to look at and warm me up.

Soon the fire was roaring nicely. The warmth felt good on my face and arms. There was a wonderful yellow glow in the room. I was beginning to feel better.

Suddenly, a tall socked figure was plodding behind me. "Gwen, I don't want to fight. Please come to bed," Linda said in a soft warm voice.

"I don't want to fight either, hon." As I spoke I pulled the blanket off the couch and put it on the floor in front of the fire. "Come on, let's sit here for a while. I'll make you some tea," I offered. Linda agreed and after I brought the tea we sat together holding each other in front of the fire.

The glow of the fire was beautiful on Linda's face. I thought, *This is such a cliche, but I love a fire. And I love the way people look when images of flame dance on them.* Feelings of deep love for Linda welled up in me as we sat there, silently.

As the warmth and glow of the fire healed us, I felt as if we were melting together. Linda's left breast pressed against my arm. I could feel her heartbeat and her slow, even breaths. At each inspiration of air, her midline flesh would gently touch my side. Then I felt Linda's warm lips as she began to kiss me on the neck behind my ear, so soft was her mouth's touch.

She slid her lips down and then forward on my neck, sending chills through my body. I shuddered visibly. I closed my eyes and focused everything on the physical sensations of the heat from the fire and her lips on my skin.

Then I felt a flicker of moisture just inside my ear. She expertly ran her tongue around the upper inside curve and then plunged the moist membrane into my ear, the end of her tongue pushing and pulling, snaking its way into me.

I felt that familiar shot of pleasure from my head to my groin, stinging me where it landed and spreading out down my inner thighs, like an electrical charge.

Linda left my ear and began kissing and sucking my shoulder. At the same time she slipped her hand under my t-shirt and began to caress my breast. Her hand felt hot as the tentacles from it squeezed and released my nipple. She lifted my t-shirt from the bottom with the other hand and moved her mouth to my other nipple. She circled it with her tongue, then put her whole mouth over it and sucked.

I was beginning to boil inside. Every part of my body was rushing with new blood. The electrical charges were coming more frequently and dwelling lower in that place before they branched out down my legs. I reached out to hold Linda's head on my breast. Both of my hands were now cradling it there, pressing her mouth against me. She sucked her way over to my left breast and continued the same flicking and drawing in of my nipple. While pulling her head against me, I leaned my head and shoulders back slightly and noises escaped from my throat.

She now forced me back on the blanket, without removing her mouth from me. She lay on top of me, her mouth still suctioned to my breast. For a long time she continued on my breasts, alternating from one to the other. Then she moved her body off mine a little, so that her back was against the fire. She ran her hand down to my crotch and began, with those hot tentacles, to squeeze and rub my clit. The electrical charge was now totally focused on that area and became more and more intense — stinging and spreading, stinging and spreading.

My buttocks began grinding into the floor in a circular motion that caused the sensation down there to mount even more. Linda brought her mouth down and switched places with her hands. Her tongue began that same flicking and sucking motion on my cunt now, and she placed one hand on each nipple, playing with them with her fingers.

The mounting sensation in my lower portion reached almost a peak of explosion, then subsided briefly. The mounting of feeling towards that peak became more intense each time and the receding briefer.

Finally, there was no receding and the peak of intense tingling, stinging, throbbing pleasure continued to rise. I was writhing now, and choking sounds rose from deep within me. My breaths were jerky in anticipation. Then, as if bubbling up from my deepest inner being, the peak rose to heights of no return and like a volcano exploded with gigantic force, wet lava bubbling out of me, the great pleasure flowing out again and again as if being drawn out to the last drop.

After several minutes my hands, which were still grasping Linda's head, pulled her gently up. She lay on top of my now rubber-like body and we rested.

After a while, I started to move under Linda. "Where are you going?" she asked with almost a hurt look on her face.

"Not far," I responded, "just to put more wood on the fire."

"Oh, I'll do that, you just stay right here," she said firmly.

I watched Linda out of the corner of my eye as she lightly removed herself from me and began putting logs on the fire. She stopped at one point and removed her pajamas, then resumed stoking. Flames burst up as she fed the fire with wood and oxygen. As they did I watched the light reflect off her long lean body and those full powerful thighs. Her buttocks flared out a bit at the bottom, making her ass look like an upside-down heart.

Her breasts were beautifully formed, high on her chest, large enough to droop just slightly. I could see little golden hairs standing up on her in the reflection of the glow, and goose bumps formed on her skin as a wave of heat flowed over her. Her face was chiseled with high cheekbones and a strong jaw. Big blue eyes with long brown lashes studied their task. Soon I wasn't certain where the glow was coming from, her or the fire. She was, indeed, radiant. I wondered why I would need anyone else. I also felt insecure. Why did she love me so much? I chided myself for the thought and was able to shove it away so as to just enjoy the moment.

When she finished her task she sat facing me, her back again to the fire. In this position the glow seemed to emanate from her like an aura.

I felt conflicting desires welling up in me. I wanted to make love to her but I didn't want to take my eyes off her whole body just as it was. I told her this.

After a moment she said, "I think I have a solution."

Still lying on my back, I reached my hand up and lightly ran my fingers over her legs and torso. She took my hand and leaning over, placed my palm over her mouth and kissed it. Then she brought her body to my hand and jammed her breast into my palm. She held the back of my hand cupped over her breast and led it to where she wanted it to go. Then she swung one leg over me so that her body was straddling my chest. She knelt in this position, and she guided both my hands through her hair, over her face, and all around her upper body. I could still see her fully, towering over me, and I wanted her badly.

She seemed to sense this and slowly edged her way up over my face, so that her legs spread wide above me. I could see in the fire glow the darkened fields of skin, the tissue of her labia, and her large protruding clitoris, still engorged.

I watched myself finger and spread her genitals, poking and pressing on her clit. Her vagina was soft and slippery as I moved my finger in and out. Linda moaned as I inserted my fingers, and she spread her legs farther, bringing herself down close to my mouth.

I spread the labia farther, with my fingers now removed from her, and licked the protruding knob firmly and slowly. "Go inside," she moaned. I entered her vagina first with my tongue, then with my fingers. With my other hand I pressed her bottom down on my fingers and into my mouth. I began to simultaneously lick her and ride my fingers in and out of her vagina. She assisted by moving herself up and down onto my fingers, her vagina slipping down over them, and then up.

I stretched my head and neck up to maintain constant contact with her clitoris while sinking my fingers in and out of her. The inside of her vagina felt hot, wet, and gloriously mushy.

Her up-and-down movements were augmented by short, sudden jerks as I continued to fuck and suck her. I could still see her torso rising and falling, welling large with deep breaths. I reached up with my free hand and massaged her breasts. "Yes, oh, yes," she began to repeat over and over, and sometimes she called my name. "Gwen, oh, yes."

My own body was on fire again as Linda and I continued our rhythmic lovemaking. Her sudden jerky movements came more frequently, and her belly seemed to swell larger and larger with each breath. She began to move faster. I accommodated by shoving my fingers in and out more rapidly and flicking her clit at a rapid speed, with my tongue contracted into a harder muscle.

The pace became frenzied, with Linda popping up and down and wriggling wildly. She pressed herself harder and harder on my fingers and mouth with each downward movement.

Suddenly she screamed out, "Oh, Gwen, I love you." Her whole body was twitching out of control. Her legs seemed to buckle under her as if she would collapse. She exuded a final, great, full-body shudder and then she stopped moving. She reached down and grasped my hand that was in her. Slowly she lifted herself up off of my hand and laid her body over me, her head hanging loosely next to mine. "Whew," she groaned, "you're the best."

I was fully satisfied. Sex and love do go together quite nicely, I thought.

We lay like that, feeling complete — inner and outer warmth — for a long time. The fire continued its dance on us.

22

For a couple of months Linda and I went along in wedded bliss. We even bought a washer and dryer. I still had my room at the nurses' residence but I didn't stay there much. And when I did it was for convenience after working late. I wasn't really tempted to see anyone else. I was busy with my relationship, work, and a new group of friends, the basketball team.

A group of women doctors, nurses, and nursing assistants from the hospital had formed a team. We practiced weekly and played against other hospital staffs during the season. It was a lot of fun.

Linda had her own activities. She had decided to start a group in Brooklyn similar to the one Sarah ran in Manhattan. It was a meditation group for lesbians and gay men.

The formation and running of the group took a lot of Linda's time. She was more than a little obsessed with this group. Starting it seemed to fulfill many of her own needs that she couldn't seem to meet any other way. Her total involvement wasn't easy on our relationship, though. As much as I enjoyed seeing Linda do something that meant so much to her, the seeds of resentment began to form in me as the group took more and more time away from us.

All during our relationship, even before we started seeing each other regularly, Linda and I knew that, as different as we were, we had something very special. We both really wanted the same basic thing: a stable loving relationship and all the things that go with that. But after a while it seemed like neither of us knew how to obtain and keep what we wanted from each other.

Things between us started to weaken subtly. I found myself staying out more. Either I was with the team or out at the bars. Linda was out too. It seemed we were moving in different directions. She tried feebly to get me involved in her group. But I was too angry at it for taking her away from me. Besides, I had my own interests.

Also, the quality of the time we did spend together began to suffer. Linda was always tired and cranky. I was always drunk and was becoming more verbally abusive. Any little negative thing she said could trigger a great rage, full of defensiveness and resentment. I couldn't tolerate the slightest criticism. And Linda was good at being critical. Her "holier-than-thou" attitude about my drinking, my spiritual life — or lack of it — and my friends and activities drove me crazy. Sometimes I'd chuckle to myself and think, *If she really knew what I'd done while in this relationship, she'd flip out!*

At any rate we were becoming more distant. I could feel something slipping away but didn't know how to stop it. And sometimes I didn't want to. I knew it was just a matter of time before I would resume my usual antics.

One night Linda and I had a real blowout. It was a vicious fight that helped push me right over the edge and fleeing back into the arms of other women.

I came home late one night so drunk that I don't remember how I got home. I was angry already when I got there — imagining the shit I'd get from Linda about my condition. Sure enough, when I came in, Linda took one look at me stumbling through the door and sneered, "God, you're a mess."

That's all it took. I began screaming. But screaming wasn't enough this time, and I began picking up furniture and dishes and smashing them on the floor. I had half destroyed the apartment when Linda, in a total panic — thinking that she was Cassius Clay and could knock me out with a punch — wound up and threw me a hard right.

It was a hell of a punch that sent me flying on my butt, but it only infuriated me more. I got up and smashed some more things, all the while screaming obscenities. Finally I fled out the door. I staggered around the streets of Brooklyn for a while. Then I went back up to the apartment and walked past Linda to the couch, where I slept it off.

The next morning, unfortunately, I woke up. I looked around and saw the destroyed apartment. Everything was still where I smashed it. And Linda was gone.

I spent the morning cleaning up my mess. I didn't know what Linda was going to do. I was scared and embarrassed but still carried a small bit of righteous indignation. Part of me thought she had it coming. I had to think that way if I was going to be able to look at myself in the mirror again. What mirror? That, too, lay smashed on the floor.

That afternoon, I called Linda at work. Her voice was cold, and at first she didn't have much to say. I didn't apologize, but I did tell her that I had cleaned up and was about to go out to replace some things. We waited in silence for a minute on each end of the line.

Then she said, "Gwen, I can't have this kind of violence in my home. I want you to know that I went to an Al-Anon meeting today. I called Tracy this morning and I told her about what happened. She insisted on taking me to a meeting." Tracy was a friend of Linda's whose lover was a recovered alcoholic.

She went on, "I learned at the meeting that I should pack a bag and leave it by the door. They said the minute things start to escalate I'm to grab that bag and go stay with someone. And that's what I'm going to have to do now."

I was so relieved that she wasn't going to leave me completely that I couldn't get angry about what she had just said. I couldn't even really take it in. I was in a bit of a shock to think she had gone to an Al-Anon meeting about me. I immediately told myself that she was overreacting. Anyway, she could pack ten bags. I knew that last night's disaster wasn't going to happen again.

"Well, I'm glad you've done whatever you thought you needed to do," I said maturely. "But it's not going to happen again."

"I hope not," she responded. "But I can't take that chance. I'm going to continue going to these meetings. Tracy said she'd go with me sometimes," she added.

"Fine," I said, acting unaffected. "Whatever you think is best for you." I remember thinking, *I hope this doesn't mean she expects me to go to A.A.* I might classify myself as a heavy drinker, but certainly not as an alcoholic.

Linda came home that night and packed her bag and put it by the door as she had promised. To me it was sort of an ominous reminder of that night, but also of what might become of our relationship.

Not much more was said about the fight except, after a while, when things had warmed up a little between us, Linda told me that to herself, she referred to it as the "night of the damned." We both laughed just a little at that. And forever more, if it ever came up, it was known as "The Night of the Damned."

Linda continued to go to Al-Anon meetings, and for a few weeks our relationship actually seemed to improve, just a little, although something new had now edged its way between us. Linda had lost trust in me. I felt badly about that, but told myself that she was overly sensitive.

And when I focused on myself, I was acutely aware of the voids in my life. I needed understanding. I needed someone who would accept me. I certainly needed someone who would be there for me. Since Linda was so busy and preoccupied, I started to look elsewhere for the attention I needed. Sarah helped a lot. But I needed more than that. I needed to feel desired by someone.

ಖ23

O nce in a while, I would attend Sarah's group at the center. Mostly I went to see her, but I also made some friends there.

I had always had a little crush on one woman who attended regularly. She was attractive — cute, you might say. She was small-statured with short, curly blonde hair. She wore glasses that were too big for her face. She had a youthfulness about her that denied her thirty-some years. And, of course, she had a wonderful smile. Her name was Sandy.

One day, after the meditation group was over, I ran into Sandy. We were making small talk when, all of a sudden, she looked at me strangely and asked, "Gwen, do you and Linda have a monogamous relationship?"

Taken aback by the unexpectedness of the question, I answered honestly. "Yeah, it's supposed to be monogamous."

"Oh," she said, with her mouth turned up a little at the corner.

Regaining my composure I questioned, "Why do you ask?"

She looked at me with a twinkle in her eyes and said, "I think that's pretty obvious."

I was stunned. "Wow," I kept saying to myself, over and over.

All that night I couldn't get Sandy out of my mind. I was so used to being on the other end of the seduction game, I wasn't sure what to make of it all.

I started going to Sarah's meetings regularly. Most of the time Sandy was there and we talked and flirted after meetings. Just when I was about to ask her out, though, she told me she was going to Europe on vacation for two weeks. Bummer, I thought. Well, it would give me time to plan my strategy.

It was the longest two weeks in history, as I awaited Sandy's return. I played basketball, worked, and hung out — without being able to get her out of my mind for a moment. At night, lying in bed next to Linda, I fantasized about making love with Sandy. I had a real case of the hots for this woman.

Finally the two weeks were over, and although I didn't see her at the meeting that week, I figured she was probably home. After the group that Sunday afternoon, I called her on the phone.

"Sandy, this is Gwen," I said nervously.

"Oh, hi, Gwen, it's nice to hear your voice," she answered sweetly.

"How was Europe?" I asked, totally uninterested.

"Oh, it was great!" she said with enthusiasm.

"Listen, Sandy," I went on, "I feel we've sort of been skirting around an issue between us. Well, you know what I mean. I feel that when you left for your vacation, things between us were left kind of hanging in the air."

"Yes," she said slowly, and a moment later, "I think it's time we brought it down to earth. Why don't you come to my place for dinner, say, tomorrow night?"

"Sounds good," I said, trying to conceal my excitement. "About seven?"

"That would be fine," she said.

"See you then," I concluded, trying to sound seductive.

I couldn't sleep that night very well. I would fall asleep for a little while, then wake up with great anxiety. I wanted this woman so badly. Finally, I had to get up and have a few shots of vodka so that I could sleep. And all the next day at work, I could think of nothing else except what was to come in a few hours. I was feeling a strange mixture of anticipation and anxiety, happiness and dread. Somehow, I thought this liaison might be what I had needed for so long. I had a fantasy that somehow Sandy would meet all of my needs.

I got out of work at my usual time. Since I wasn't meeting Sandy until seven, I had time to kill. Sandy lived in a small studio apartment in Harlem. I decided to walk north on Columbus Avenue to her place.

As I was walking, the anxiety became almost unbearable. A strange fixation kept nagging me. *What if I run into someone I know in Harlem? What am I going to say about what I'm doing there? I don't know anyone in Harlem except Sandy, and I can't say I'm going there to see her. Linda can't find out about this. That would really put the icing on the cake.* Worry, worry, that thought kept at me. My pace quickened as I racked my brain trying to think of a plausible reason for being in Harlem. I knew there were always festivals going on, but damned if I knew where or what they were.

Suddenly, as if a voice came from somewhere else, my reasoning ability snapped into place. My mind said, *If you don't know anyone in Harlem, how can you run into anyone you know in Harlem? Oh, yeah,* I thought. *Who would be there to catch me?*

Relieved from that obsession, I could focus on what I was really anxious about. What was going to happen tonight? Was she going to think I was a good lover? Would this satisfy my current needs? What was going to happen tonight?

I reached Sandy's apartment early. I probably set a record for walking twenty city blocks in five minutes. I rang her bell anyway, thinking she might be home. No luck! I looked around the neighborhood, hoping to find a bar with a reasonable mix of men and women, but there was only a coffee shop. It was perfect. I could sit at the counter by the entrance and watch her front door. That way I would see her when she got home.

I settled in at the counter, checked my position to be sure I could see her door, and ordered a cup of tea. I sat sipping and scanning. My hold on the tea cup was a little shaky. I was deep in thought and bursting with eagerness. I think I might have been mumbling to myself, inaudibly.

Then out of nowhere came this voice: "Gwen! What the hell are you doing in Harlem?" I swung around toward the voice on my left and there in the doorway of the coffee shop stood Corky, an old friend of mine. She bore a very quizzical expression.

I couldn't believe it. "Well — uh, I'm, uh, waiting, uh, for someone," I spat out. "What are you doing here?" I asked her back.

"I'm working for the visiting nurses and I have some patients to see in this area," she responded.

"Oh," I said sheepishly.

Corky sat down beside me, still with a question on her face. Since she had been a pretty close friend, and I was about to jump out of my skin anyway, I told her everything. After I stopped talking, she continued to study me with her mouth open and an "uh-huh" look in her eyes.

"Can I come too?" she asked, after a minute.

"No way!" I admonished. "You're nuts. I'm having a hard enough time without you being there."

She smiled, because she knew I wasn't going to go for that, and said, "Damn, it sounds like fun."

"Well, I think for today you'll have to find your own fun," I said, firmly but warmly.

"I guess I should be going," she said, still with that look in her eyes. "Let me know how it works out."

"Right," I said, as if I meant it. "See ya later." (Much later, I hoped.)

Moments after Corky left, I saw Sandy standing at her front door, holding a bag of groceries. I jumped up from my stool and met her at her door.

"Hi," I said, "I was early so I had a cup of tea across the street. You wouldn't believe the bizarre thing that happened just now!" As we walked up the stairs I filled Sandy in on Corky's surprise visit. She thought it was very funny.

Sandy's apartment was small and had very little furniture. Just some wall hangings, a few plants, some bookcases, and a rug. She motioned to me to have a seat on the floor. She informed me, "I like sitting on the floor and that's where we'll be eating." I scanned the area for a bed and noted a blue futon mattress, tucked away over in a corner of the room.

I sat, a little stiffly, on the floor while watching Sandy prepare dinner in her little kitchenette. It was hard to get the conversation going. I didn't know how to start. She took over.

"Oh, I want to show you some pictures of my trip," she said. She brought in a bunch of pictures and handed them to me. While she cooked, I looked. I noticed that two men and one woman showed up frequently in the pictures.

"Who are these people?" I asked finally. She came over and, pointing at the faces, said, "These two are my friends that I went to visit. They're married. And this is Zak. I met him through them. The four of us spent the whole two weeks together."

Why was I beginning to get a sick feeling in the pit of my stomach?

We made small talk while she completed the dinner. After she sat down and we began eating, I felt it was time to put the cards out on the table.

"You know," I started, "ever since you asked me at the center about monogamy, I felt that we have been kind of heading toward getting together. To be honest, I've thought about it a lot and really would like to have a physical relationship with you."

Sandy paused and then with an expression of excitement and innocence said, "Yeah, I know that's been kind of there. But there's something I have to tell you. You see, while I was in Europe, I met this guy, the one in the picture, Zak. And — well, I've fallen deeply in love with him. In fact, I'm here now only to pack my stuff. I'm going right back to move in with him."

My stomach at once turned into a rock and, for a moment, I thought I was going to throw up on Sandy's dinner. I couldn't speak, so I didn't. Sandy went on, "I never thought this would be possible. But he's so wonderful, Gwen. I've never felt this strongly for anyone. And I just know it's going to work out. I'm already training him how to make love to me. You know how self-centered men can be in that area."

At this point I was totally speechless. I thought, *You're training him to make love to you? How stupid! Why don't you just find someone who already knows how to do it, like a woman!* But I continued to listen.

It was really hard to hide my disappointment, but somehow I managed to convince Sandy that I was happy for her. I chomped down dinner, squeezing it into the small knot that was now my stomach. As soon as I could gracefully exit, I did.

Sandy insisted on walking me to the subway. As we walked in the cool air of early fall, she topped off the evening by saying, "You know, I am attracted to you. Maybe someday we could get together."

I felt a wild impulse to punch her right in the face, but smiled instead and said, "Yeah, maybe someday. Keep me in mind."

With a quick thanks for dinner and good luck, I was finally free from her. I got on the subway and sat down. I felt all of my energy gone. I was drained, disappointed, disgusted, and depressed.

I wanted to be alone. I decided to go back to my room at the nurses' residence for the night. I stopped first to buy myself a fifth of vodka. When I got to my room, I poured myself a large drink and called Linda. I made some excuse about why I was staying at the room. She tried briefly to talk me into coming home but gave up easily when she realized I wasn't going to budge.

After hanging up the phone I quickly chugged the liquor and poured some more. I was still depressed but the liquor soon began to ease the pain. After a while I passed out on the bed. All thoughts and feelings were, for a brief time, sent into oblivion.

24

For a few days I dragged myself around feeling sorry for myself and feeling stupid. Then the depression began to lift and I set my mind free of Sandy and resumed my usual course of action. I figured in time someone would come along who would make me feel better.

I didn't have to wait long. A woman I knew from Gabriel's bar had been after me for a while. I had put her off because I was only mildly attracted to her and my attention had been on Sandy. But now things were different. I wanted a sure thing.

So one night, a week after my fiasco with Sandy, I went to Gabriel's. Mary Ann was there as usual. We sat at the bar together and got pretty tanked. In my drunkenness I told her about Sandy. She agreed that the woman won the Jerk of the Year award.

As the evening progressed, Mary Ann became more and more desirable. She really was nice-looking. It wasn't her looks that had previously dismayed me, but a quality of clinginess in her personality that had turned me off. But tonight she was taking care of me. And that's what I wanted. So after we both acquired a hefty buzz, I asked her to come back to my room with me. She agreed immediately, and we set off to my lair.

On the way we stopped and picked up a half-gallon of wine. Mary Ann also informed me that she had some pot on her.

"All right!" I said, "Let's party tonight."

As soon as we reached our destination, we popped open the wine and lit a joint. The night took on a festive atmosphere and soon we were whooping it up, without any cares or woes.

Our lovemaking began quickly and without any thought. All I knew is we soon had our clothes off and Mary Ann was kissing me hard and passionately. She was aggressive, and I momentarily found myself lying back on the bed with her scrambling on top of me, kissing and sucking everything. It was difficult to have an orgasm under all the booze and pot, but with Mary Ann's persistence, my body managed to squeeze one out.

After our calisthenics, we took a break for another joint and more wine. It was then she informed me that she was on medication for depression and, consequently, had a very hard time having orgasms.

"I guess my work is cut out for me then," I said lightly, and we both laughed hysterically in drunken abandonment.

In my drunken grandiosity, I was undaunted by this information and approached Mary Ann with an air of total confidence. I told her, "With me you'll have an orgasm." She was a believer.

She pulled me down over her and I immediately began pursuing every erotic zone I knew. I squeezed and kneaded her lower buttocks, pressed and rubbed the pressure points of her back and neck. I sucked on her breasts, the inside of her thighs, and ate away at her genitals. I massaged her G-spot with my fingers. I played my tongue in and out of every orifice. I worked and worked on her tiny body, tirelessly.

At times it seemed she was close. She would moan and groan, indicating release, and then lose it. She told me to keep going. And I did. After countless times of getting close to that great bursting point and failing, Mary Ann began to get upset. After one episode of rising almost to the orgasmic flow, then losing it again, she began to scream out wildly, "I want an orgasm! I want an orgasm!"

Instantly I stopped and said firmly, "Mary Ann, please, they can hear you! Not so loud."

But my warning had no effect on her, and she continued to scream louder and louder: "I want an orgasm!!"

I stopped completely and sat up at the side of the bed. I poured us both another glass of wine, hoping that that would calm her down. She grabbed the glass from my hand and stood on the bed. With both arms outstretched and wine flying out of the glass clenched in her hand, she screamed at the top of her lungs: "I WANT AN ORGASM!"

By this time I was sure every nurse from three floors was probably outside my door laughing hysterically — or worse, totally freaked out.

I finally managed to calm Mary Ann down a little. She agreed to sit on the bed but continued mumbling those words quietly under her breath.

All of a sudden I heard a tremendous commotion in the hall outside my room. Someone had let out a howl and then we heard a loud thumping noise.

I looked at Mary Ann and said, "What's that?!"

She seemed to snap out of her stupor and said, "I don't know — let's go see."

I agreed and got up to find my clothes. I was snapping my jeans on when I turned and saw Mary Ann heading out the door — naked. She had forgotten her clothes.

I yelled after her, "Mary Ann, you don't have any clothes on!" It was to no avail. She whisked herself out the door and into the hall.

As soon as I could throw on my t-shirt, I ran after her. A small crowd of women had formed outside my room around someone who had collapsed. There amidst them stood Mary Ann, staring at the woman on the floor. Everyone else was staring at Mary Ann. I grabbed her arm and said sternly, "Go back and put your clothes on!"

She blinked, looked down at herself, up at the crowd, let out a squeal, and then scurried back into the room.

I stayed just a few minutes to see if I could be of assistance, but there were plenty of nurses around already. I went back to the room still wondering what had happened, shaking off a horrible thought that it had something to do with us.

Mary Ann and I were sobered by the episode. We climbed in bed and talked for a short time about what we thought might have happened to the woman. We fell asleep still not knowing.

The next day on my way to work, I asked someone in the hall if they had heard about the woman. I was told that someone had just fainted and that it wasn't serious. I was glad for the woman, but that lingering question plagued me. I finally dismissed my worries, thinking, *Oh well — at least she's all right.*

❧25

I went home that evening after work, exhausted from the previous evening's antics. It was good to be with Linda even though she got home late. The small amount of time we spent together before going to bed felt so sane. As I lay beside her that night, I thought again about what I had in our relationship. Maybe what I was looking for to fulfill certain needs wasn't out there anymore. Maybe it never had been.

I noticed over the next few weeks that Linda seemed more preoccupied than ever about her work with the meditation group. I still didn't want to get involved but I didn't feel as resentful as before. I saw how much this project was draining her in a way, but also giving her new energy. She was brighter and often more outgoing than I had ever seen her.

Sometimes she would talk about the different people who came to her group. Some were helping her with the work, and some were just plain in crisis. She would ask my advice about them. I realized when she talked about them that I couldn't even put names to faces. I didn't know these people at all.

And similarly, when I talked with Linda about members of the basketball team, she responded as if I were talking about strangers. She didn't know them either. Our lives were getting further apart. We were spending our time in two different communities.

I still believed that this was okay. I saw no reason we couldn't have our own separate lives and be together, too. But I could see it was a little harder on Linda, not having me around at the very least to support her emotionally. She would sometimes, in her subtle way, seek out my support. I usually found ways to push her aside, thinking, This is her thing and she's going to have to manage it herself.

So during these days we came together for brief periods, each of us preoccupied with our own separate lives. Our being together sometimes felt like a convenience. Deep down I think we knew that our love was still strong. But maybe we were putting too many things in the way of that love. We allowed everything else to take priority in our lives. We allowed our relationship to drift apart.

We began to have a hard time listening to each other's feelings, and after a while we shared less and less with each other. I knew we weren't doing justice to our relationship, if I really thought about it. But I figured it was probably the way most relationships went. And I convinced myself that the security and home it provided was enough.

If Linda was more dissatisfied, she didn't let me know it.

≈ 26

The basketball team consisted of about eight of us regulars, with a few women straggling in and out as their schedules would permit. We called each other by nicknames. As soon as one became a regular player she was given a nickname befitting her abilities, or sometimes her personality.

There was Deadeye, a tall, blonde, vivacious woman who was co-captain and, of course, an incredible shot. The Whip was also co-captain; she was small in stature but, you guessed it, whipped around the court with speed and agility. There was Bam, a tall slim beauty with long, wild black hair. If you happened to bump into Quick, a sturdy, muscular being who could sink one from midcourt, it felt like you were hitting a stone wall. Zoey was a large, heavy woman who moved with incredible grace on the court, had phenomenal moves under the basket, and could slip the ball right into the hoop before you knew what had happened. She also had the sweetest disposition. Row was smooth. Everything about her was smooth, the way she played ball and the way she lived her life. She was dark and beautiful. Lou was a tall, full-figured woman, a little clumsy on the court but with potential. Subway could really move the ball. She was an incredible and versatile player who joined us after the first season.

And they called me Wildwoman. I was an adequate player — a good shot. My drinking and smoking slowed me down a little.

We tried to practice twice a week. During the season sometimes we were at it three nights a week. After our practices or games, we would go out together to eat and drink beer. Sometimes we did other social things together. Deadeye and Bam were very active and frequently proposed different activities for us all to join in on. We went to tennis tournaments and concerts and fairs. Sometimes we had parties — Bam loved a party. Bam even had a seder every year at her apartment for her friends.

The team rapidly became my main social group. I secretly had crushes on different members at different times. Some of the women were straight. That made it even more intriguing.

This year Deadeye proposed an incredible adventure to kick off the season. She said she thought a wonderful way to bring us all together would be to take a ski trip to Colorado. Her parents had a condominium in Winter Park and would love to have us for a few days. Deadeye was an expert cross-country skier, whose mother supposedly could ski anything. I had never been skiing in my life. But Deadeye assured me that with my athletic nature, I could pick it up fast.

Many of us from the team joyously accepted the invitation and agreed to make time to go on the trip. I even asked Linda if she wanted to join us, but she said no. She said she didn't really know anyone and, besides, she couldn't leave her newly formed group for that many days.

I looked forward with great excitement to the trip. I had never been to Colorado. And the thought of staying in the mountains and skiing for the first time thrilled me.

&27

The day finally arrived for the big trip to Colorado. It was late fall and there was still no snow in New York. But Deadeye reassured us that there was plenty in Colorado. Her mother had reported a fresh snowfall just that week. So all systems were go.

Not everyone who had originally agreed to go actually was able to make the trip, but there was a nice small group of people who enjoyed one another. Lou, Whip, Bam, Zoey, myself, and, of course, Deadeye boarded the plane that day.

The flight was a long one. But that was fine with us. Everyone was in a really good mood. I kept trying to imagine what skiing was going to be like. I asked Deadeye questions about the condo and the mountains. She just said, "You'll see," with a twinkle in her eye.

Deadeye's mom and dad picked us up at the airport. They were both so friendly and welcoming, it felt as if we were coming home after a long journey. We went to their house in Denver for lunch, then Deadeye and her mom drove the brood up into the mountains to the condo.

As we drove, the scenery became more and more mountainous. The peaks of snow-filled Rockies surrounded us. The beauty became greater and the wilderness more vast as we drove on. Deadeye's mom finally selected a mountain, and we began the trip upward. She mentioned that just a few days earlier we might not have been able to get up this mountain because of a snowstorm.

We wound our way up and around the mountain. Soon we could see only their tops and sharp peaks. At one point, Deadeye's mother pointed at a particularly high peak and said, "A couple of years ago there was an avalanche from there. It covered the road in very deep snow." A shiver ran down my spine at the thought of it, but also a fun thought occurred to me. Maybe we could get snowed in!

Then out of the wilderness appeared, in the near distance, a housing complex. We drove to the outer edge of the complex, where the condo was. Deadeye's condo was on the very end of a small row of apartments. We lugged our stuff inside.

The condo had a small living room and kitchen, two bedrooms, and a fireplace. It was decorated in New Mexican style. Just outside the door was a wooden railing and beyond that, to our right, wilderness. To our left the community of the complex bustled.

I thought at first that a solitary cabin might be even nicer, until I realized the perks of the complex. It had two indoor swimming pools, indoor hot tubs, and a horse-drawn sleigh. Nothing like combining the beauty of the wilderness with all the creature comforts, I thought.

As we settled in, Deadeye started a fire and her mom prepared supper. We spent the evening talking, reading, and playing games around the fire. Periodically I would go outside by the banister and look into the dark wilderness. A thought came to me that repeated itself throughout my stay: *I wish Linda could see this.*

The next day we arose early to get a good start on the day. We ate a small breakfast at the condo while Deadeye packed for our cross-country trip: cheese, salami, fruit, and some peach liqueur. We were instructed how to dress and to take plenty of water. She fitted us for skis and poles. They even had extra hats and mittens there in their well-stocked condo. I was amazed at how prepared they were to outfit people.

Deadeye's final suggestion was that we bring a couple of sleeping bags to carry on our backs. She said it was for safety; if we had any trouble we would have extra warmth. Also they would be good to sit on during breaks. I volunteered to take one and Deadeye took the other.

We then drove to one of the main downhill skiing areas, which had cross-country trails adjacent to it. The course was about seven miles long, Deadeye said. She consoled us begin-ners by saying that she would teach us as we went along how to manage the steep and winding spots and how to go uphill on skis. The flatter areas would be easy.

Off we went. Some of the more experienced of our group seemed to almost disappear as they pulled ahead quickly in their exuberance. I stumbled along. At first the big long sticks on my feet were cumbersome. After a short while I had no problem with the even stroking and sliding on the flatter surfaces. But the downhill parts were killers.

I couldn't slow the skis down enough to maneuver the twists and turns at the bottoms of the hills. Time after time I went flying into deep snowdrifts on the sides of the trail. Soon I was covered from head to toe with snow. Deadeye was patient, and instructed me over and over how to slow down and how to turn. She had the patience of a saint. With every little improvement, she showered me with praise. But, alas, even so, by the time we sat down for lunch, I was exhausted and bathed in snow.

We stopped for lunch on a ridge overlooking a valley below and mountains in the distance. The sky was a piercing blue. The sun was high. We ate and drank and rested in the splendor of the creation. The sun was warm, reflecting off the white, white snow. Except for the wind through the trees, there was silence all around us.

After eating and resting, it was time to resume our journey. Deadeye told us that we were about to confront a very long decline. She told the experienced ones just to go ahead, that she would guide the rest of us.

Off again went most of our group. A couple of us dragged behind trying to maneuver this torturous slope. I spent a great deal of time in the snow, headfirst. But I thought finally that I was beginning to get the idea. I was able to gracefully accomplish some of the less steep portions of the decline. But the going was slow and I was lagging behind. I would study each section to make a plan before proceeding. That was helping me stay on my feet, but it was slowing me down considerably.

Deadeye would ski ahead and then come back to check on me. I counted on seeing her smiling face periodically.

I was moving along quite nicely when I came to a steep drop. I stopped dead in my tracks. A yellow caution sign with a big exclamation mark in the middle was nailed to a tree at the top where I stood. I looked down and saw a mean twist at the bottom of the hill. At this point I looked around me and realized I was completely alone. I hadn't seen Deadeye now for quite some time. I knew the others must be far ahead. The thought ran through my mind that they'd all gotten tired of my slowness and decided to leave me to my own fate.

As I stood at the top of this winding, steep, treacherous hill, my eyes alternating between my journey and that sign, I thought, *Well, I have two choices. I can go down the hill, or I can freeze to death.* I chose to go down the hill.

I planned my strategy as best I could. I began to make my way down by sitting on my poles in between my legs to slow me down, as Deadeye had taught me. But even so, I began gaining too much speed. I whisked around the first few curves successfully. But then the hill became even steeper, and I was soon going much too fast to safely maneuver the final hard turn at the bottom. I saw it coming, but try as I might, I couldn't slow down. When I reached the bottom and the turn, I was flying. I tried to lean as much as I could to make the curve. But nature wasn't going to give me this one.

Bam! My skis went up and over a mound of snow, and my body went flying into a large snow-covered bush. I landed with my skis going in one direction and my legs going in another. My head and trunk were buried in the bush.

When I regained full consciousness, I felt a severe pain in my right ankle. It was twisted, with the ski still on. I couldn't reach my feet with my hands because of the position of my body. I kept straining to reach the ski to unlatch it and free my foot, but my attempts were futile. After several tries I fell back in exhaustion, crying and laughing from the pain and frustration, and screaming obscenities at the situation.

When I fell back, my eyes rested on a mark in the snow. It was a large cat print. *Oh great,* I thought, *now I'm going to be somebody's lunch!*

I continued to stretch my hand down to try to unlatch my ski. The pain was becoming unbearable. Finally I managed to shift my body a little and grabbed with the tips of my fingers the bar that held my ski on, flipping it open. Gently I removed my foot and turned it from its twisted position into the correct alignment.

When the pain subsided a little, I stretched and moved my foot slowly, checking for injuries. Miraculously enough, there didn't appear to be any serious damage.

As I sat in the bush collecting myself, I heard a distant voice calling my name. "Gwen. Gwen, where are you?"

I called back, "I'm here in a bush. Deadeye? I'm here." I stood up and put pressure on my foot. It seemed okay now, the pain almost gone. I collected the skis and poles and moved back out onto the trail.

From there I could see Deadeye's robust figure skiing toward me. I stood motionless until she arrived. When she faced me, her radiant figure stood out in contrast to the surrounding environment. Even in my dazed state, I felt her physical presence. Her long golden hair was neatly fixed into a single braid that fell down her back. Her facial features had been sculpted without any over- or undersized part. Her complexion was ruddy and flushed with the color of health and outdoor exposure.

She was ageless. I thought briefly, as I examined her, that she had probably been about thirty years old all of her life. Her eyes were a pale blue. Something old was behind them. She could have been a tall tree, beautiful and sturdy — perfectly formed, yet with no single feature that stood out from the rest.

"Where were you?" she said, winded.

"Well, until a few minutes ago I was trying to come down that hill." I realized as I spoke that my body looked like a giant snowball. "I had a little trouble slowing down toward the bottom and I couldn't make that curve."

My face must have shown my fear and dismay as I spoke because Deadeye's expression took on one of great sympathy. She put her arms around me and held me for a few moments. Her body felt good, so close to mine. I felt like she was breathing some of her vigor and life into me.

She said, "Let's rest for a while." She took the sleeping bag off her back while I looked around for mine. Finally, I discovered it near the bushes where I had landed.

"Bring it over here," she commanded. I brought it over to her obediently and she said, "Let's zip them together. Our body heat together in one bag will help warm us."

I thought mischievously, *You bet it will.*

She zipped the bags together and found a smooth place under a tree a little off the trail. I slipped off my snow-covered outer layer of clothes. We got into the bag and propped ourselves up in a sitting position against the tree.

We sat there not saying much, just taking in the freshness and beauty surrounding us. I noticed the sun was beginning to drop in the sky and I worried a little about the time. "D," I said, "how much farther is the trail? It looks like it will be dark in a couple of hours."

"Don't worry," she assured me, "it's not much farther. And there's just one more rough spot."

"Well, I refuse to fall anymore," I said with conviction.

She gave me a sweet motherly smile and put her arm around my shoulders.

Deadeye had always intrigued me. She was totally competent, hard-working, talented, energetic, full of life, and willing to try anything. She told us wonderful stories of travels to faraway places. She would do things for the experience of it that few others would try.

I didn't know what her sexuality was. Sometimes she seemed like a spirit that had no gender. And sometimes she seemed all woman. She wasn't much of a talker, but spoke through her ability to reach out to people quietly, to make people feel included. She believed in simple kindness and complete justice. She was the kind of person about whom one could truly say, she could not be captured or held down. She had wings.

As we sat there in our wilderness nook, her arm still around me, I felt a tremendous peace. I could stay there forever. I had no needs, no fears, no worries. The earth seemed to cradle us there in her arms, telling us that we were part of her — part of the splendor around us.

We didn't speak for a long, long time. Then, as naturally as clinging icicles on a tree slowly drip away in the heat of the sun, Deadeye turned her face toward mine and kissed me. It was a deep and tender kiss. I wasn't surprised or challenged. It just seemed like the natural order of things. The touching of our bodies was tremendously sensual and moving, and yet without a sexual quality. It was just the culmination of two people being together at a particular moment in time, circumstance, and place that made us one. One not just with each other, but with all that was around us: the snow, the rocks, the scrub pines, the mountains, the clouds, and the sun.

When our lips parted, D said softly, "Gwen, you know that maneuver I showed you to slow yourself down?"

"Yeah," I said foggily.

"Well, it doesn't always work."

"Oh, yeah," I said, still out of it.

Deadeye began to giggle. I snapped out of my trance and realized the irony of what she had just said. I started giggling too, and soon we were laughing uproariously, rolling around in the bags.

"That way only works for moderately steep hills," she spit out, still laughing. "There's another thing I've got to show you for really steep hills."

"Okay," I coughed out, "maybe next time."

"No," Deadeye said, suddenly more seriously, "you're going to need it now."

"Oh, no," I said, falling back in the snow.

Deadeye and I got up to finish the trail. She showed me the steep-hill maneuver of pointing my skis in, toe-to-toe, and bending my ankles in so that the skis were up on their edges a little.

We went along together, for a while on a very straight plane. She was a bit ahead of me. Then she pulled farther ahead and I thought, *Oh no, don't leave me!* But soon she was a speck. Then she vanished. I continued my striding, enjoying the fun of gliding over the trail. I turned an innocent-looking bend and then, without much warning, was face-to-face with a wide, steep hill.

Down at the bottom stood the whole group, including Deadeye, waiting and watching. I stopped a moment, practiced the maneuver I had just learned, and then proceeded with the plunge downward. The tension in me rose to a full body knot when I went over the final lip and began my downward plummet. Skis pointed, ankles in, I slid down slowly, in control of myself. My skis crossed themselves twice, but I compensated and got them to respond to my command. Just before reaching the bottom, I looked up and saw Deadeye beaming from ear to ear with a thumb pointed high in the air.

When I reached bottom the group cheered and applauded. I felt terrific. I couldn't put it into words, but somehow I knew that I had been changed — that I was a slightly better person than I had been that morning.

28

By the time we got back to the condo, it was dark. I still felt exhilarated, even though my body was wet and aching.

Zoey and Quick cooked dinner and we ate Mexican food by the fire. Downhill skiing was planned for the next day. Feeling like I had just completed a course in Outward Bound, I was frightened at the thought of downhill. But I still wanted to try it, and the spirit of my difficult but successful day lingered.

After dinner, as we cleaned up our dishes, someone asked about the swimming pools. Deadeye said, "Yeah, that's a great idea. Let's go for a swim and a soak in the jacuzzi. That'll soothe everyone's aching bones."

That sounded so good to me! We quickly donned bathing suits, put a layer of heavy clothes over them and walked the brief distance to the pool house. We undressed in the locker room and made our entrance into a room with two large pools and two large hot tubs. Hardly anyone was there. Just one woman was swimming and a couple of people were lingering in the tubs.

I wanted to take a swim to stretch out my muscles. I plunged into the pool and began stroking my way back and forth. The water felt good on my abused body. Zoey, Quick, and Whip jumped in behind me. Deadeye and Bam went straight for the hot tubs. Lou was bringing up the rear, joining us in the pool.

After swimming methodically for a while, we began playing in the pool. Someone suggested a game of tag. It was fun and soon the pool was resounding with shrieks of laughter. We didn't take long to tire, though, and soon, one by one, we got out of the pool to join Deadeye and Bam. I was the last to leave the pool.

Now for the hot tub, I thought, as I pulled my dripping body out of the pool. With water still in my eyes, I walked toward the hot tub. It was near a big glass window in the front of the building so you could see outside a little. Lights inside the tub created an aqua glow.

I reached the tub ready to jump in. As I wiped water from my eyes, I noticed some wet rags by the side of the tub. My eyes fully cleared now, and I saw that everyone was nude in the tub. Those rags were their bathing suits.

Even though I was trying to conceal my surprise and act cool, my face must have betrayed something, because soon everyone was laughing.

"Gosh, I didn't think you were such a prude, Wildwoman," Bam said with a sarcastic lilt in her voice. "Maybe we gave you the wrong name," she added.

"No, no," I said, recovering. "You guys are too much, though." I peeled off my own suit to the hurrahs of my audience and slipped into the tub.

As I settled in, the hot tub felt perfect. The hot water bubbled up and over my body, massaging all those aches and pains. I let out a big sigh and totally relaxed. "This does feel great without a suit," I murmured. I leaned my head back and closed my eyes, taking in the sense of total relaxation. As I lay there I felt a flush of well-being and thought to myself: *What a great trip this has been.* I thought fleetingly again of Linda and about what she was missing.

A sudden disconcerting yet intriguing question occurred to me. I asked Deadeye, "Is your mother coming over?"

"No, I don't think so," Deadeye answered. "She's not much for these tubs."

"Oh," I said, a little relieved and a little disappointed. I was disappointed because Deadeye's mom was beautiful. Lou already had developed a mad crush on her. "She probably wouldn't go for the nudity, huh?" I asked.

"Are you kidding? Her mother would jump right in without giving it a second thought," Bam informed me. "Now, my mother would be trudging home on foot, dragging her bags behind her," Bam joked. We all laughed at that image.

Totally relaxed, I drifted into nothingness. I heard in the background Lou and her analytical mind breaking down all the aspects of proper skiing with Deadeye. Then I vaguely heard Deadeye telling one of her stories — something about getting lost once on a hiking trip and actually having to spend the night in the woods in the rain without any of the proper equipment.

But I was in my own world, taking in all the wonderful sensations of hot bubbling water softly caressing my most hidden muscles, and daydreaming about my day's victory.

Then all voices ceased. We all wallowed silently in the delight of the tub. I guessed that everyone was lost in her own thoughts.

We were now alone in the pool area. It was getting late. Someone must have thought the place was empty, and before we knew what was happening — clink — the lights went out. The only lights remaining were the ones emanating from the jacuzzi. The whole room took on its aqua glow.

I sat up immediately and said, "Do you think we'll get locked in?"

Deadeye said calmly, "No, they never lock anything around here."

"Oh, this is better than ever," said Whip. "Look, the whole room is green."

Bam added, "This is terrific!"

Then Deadeye swished over and squeezed herself in between me and Zoey. I didn't know what she had in mind but I thought maybe she wanted to talk to me. "Yes, Doctor?" I said, with a sarcastic lilt in my voice.

But she said nothing, and settled back in the tub next to me with a small smile on her face.

Momentarily, amidst the pulsating water bubbles, I thought for a moment that I felt something else. Yes, there was something else. Deadeye had put her hand on my upper leg and was stroking it.

At that point I looked at her. She was looking straight ahead, her mouth curved into a slight smile. At the same time I noticed her other hand was stretched out on the other side a little. I leaned forward and caught Zoey's face. Zoey returned my gaze and brought her eyes down to indicate she too was being stroked.

Part of me wanted to burst out laughing at Deadeye's outrageousness. But part of me was also a little nervous and excited about what I thought was about to happen.

I took my cue from Deadeye and reached out to her firm, muscular leg and began the same stroking back and forth. At times we would join hands under the water and clasp and squeeze them together. Then we went back to the stroking.

Quick sat on my other side. I began with my other hand the same stroking of her leg. At first she jumped a little. Then she looked at all three of us, and seemed quickly to get the message. She soon returned the favor and began stroking my other leg.

At this moment a concern welled up in me. I could see clearly now where we were going. I wasn't at all sure about how Whip and Bam would react. I was pretty sure they were straight. I watched, somewhat ill at ease, as the circle of stroking hands made its way over to them.

When Lou got to Bam, Bam didn't seem to flinch or hesitate to join in. But when Whip, the final person, was engaged, she let out a yelp and with a start, jumped out of the tub. Apparently she hadn't been aware of anything going on until it got to her. Her face was red as she grabbed her suit and ran towards the locker room.

At that point all our underwater activity stopped. I think we all felt badly about embarrassing Whip. Deadeye mumbled something about not wanting to do anything that would make someone feel left out. We sat there quietly for a few minutes. I know I was more than a little disappointed.

Apparently Whip had gone into the locker room and collected her thoughts. She came back into the room, walking slowly toward us. When she reached the tub she looked down at us and said profoundly, "Oh, what the hell!" With that, she plunged into the middle of the tub and came up with her head between Bam's legs. *Boy,* I thought. *When she makes a decision, she really makes a decision!*

Whip returned to her place in between Bam and Zoey. Our hands immediately resumed slipping over one another's legs. Now with more conviction, we were exploring the flesh under the green-blue bubbles.

Deadeye again took the lead. She moved her hand up my leg to my crotch and softly ran her fingers around my mound, dipping over and into my labia. I responded by doing the same to her and to Quick.

Soon the members of the circle were again in unison, slipping and sliding their fingers around and into one another's genitals. After a few minutes of this, some of us began squirming. The water grew more turbulent with our movements.

Next, I took the lead. Quick was sitting so her right breast was exposed above the water. I leaned my head down and began licking her nipple. Soon, everyone followed and began tonguing her neighbor's breast.

After this addition the movements of our bodies became even more pronounced. I was totally turned on. What the bubbling hot water was not able to accomplish, these deft fingers and mouths were!

Deadeye began to concentrate her fingers on my clit. She rubbed it back and forth, squishing and releasing it. Soon we were all doing the same to one another, continuing our breast sucking.

We pursued these motions for a long time. My own body was rising in excitement from the physical manipulations, the perceivable arousal of five others moving and moaning, and the persistent bubbling of hot water over us.

My body began to respond with that familiar rise as it began its agitation toward orgasm. Deadeye's fingers were squeezing and rubbing me more intensely. Our sucking and licking became more and more lusciously uninhibited.

I moved into another consciousness in which I was overwhelmed by loud sucking noises, intense bodily sensations, and that aura of blue-green color and those bubbles and jets of water streaming and bursting upon me.

Just as I thought I was about to come, I heard a loud groan from someone. Almost simultaneously a large bubble burst on the surface. My excitement increased even more when I heard another loud moan and saw another bubble burst. Then, as if by chain reaction, everyone seemed to come one by one. Low moans surfaced from deep within us, rising to our throats. In the same way, the water, churning up from the bottom, in one gigantic bubble, from the depths of the pool, broke loose on the surface. Gurgle, gurgle, gurgle, POP!

Momentarily and almost simultaneously everyone let out great sighs. Our bodies seemed to melt together into one great gob of flesh in the tub. I sank down, my head almost submerged, and with eyes half-open, watched through the green-blue steam the persistent little blurbs of water form and fizz.

29

*T*he next day we all went downhill skiing. I wasn't bad for my first time. And again, being out there with the mountains all around us in the clean crisp air was invigorating.

That night we went to a local nightclub and drank and danced. Deadeye's mother came with us and partied us under the table.

No one said anything about our jacuzzi escapade. Perhaps we were afraid it would somehow change things. Or maybe there just wasn't anything to say.

When we boarded the plane for home, I carried with me a lot of feelings. I felt renewed and optimistic about life in general. I felt ready to put some real time and effort into my relationship with Linda. I hoped I could communicate effectively to her some of my new enthusiasm.

I was even willing to cut down on my drinking, if that would help. Maybe I could attend her meditation group once in a while. I suspected I'd been shutting her out a little. One thing I knew about Linda. She was always willing to try again. She was loyal and trustworthy. She worked hard for what she wanted. If I was willing to give just a little more, she would respond in kind.

The closer we came to New York, the more enthusiastic I became to share with Linda some of what she, unfortunately, had missed.

I arrived home about ten o'clock at night. Linda was there sitting at the kitchen table. I popped in and greeted her warmly.

Without unpacking, I sat down immediately at the table and began to tell her about my experiences. I told her about the beauty, about skiing, about the lovingness of Deadeye's family. I told her I had grown from the experience of being with these generous, loving people in Denver, with nature and the earth, and with the team. I shared with her the fun of skiing and told her about the many times I wished she had been there too. I didn't tell her about the jacuzzi episode, though I wished I could.

As I was talking effusively, I was aware of a feeling of distance from Linda. She was somewhere else. Her eyes looked off into space a lot. Her face was somber. I began to feel frustrated, because I couldn't engage her in my conversation. My positiveness seemed to be bouncing off of her like a wall.

Finally, I stopped telling my story. I looked at her for a moment and asked, "Linda, is something the matter?"

"No," she responded, "I'm just tired." She went on briskly, "You know, you can't expect me to be in the same place you are right now. You always seem to expect that when you feel something I'm going to feel it too, just automatically."

"No," I argued, "I don't expect you to feel exactly the way I do. I'm just trying to tell you that I think I can change a little. I think maybe I can be more giving and loving now."

"Well, that's good," she said unenthusiastically. Then suddenly, "Look, I hope you don't mind, I'm really tired, I'm going to go to bed."

"Okay," I said, resigned but a little unsettled and angry. "I guess I'll go to bed too."

I lay next to Linda. I couldn't fall asleep. Something was nagging me. I stared at the ceiling wondering what it was. Linda seemed so distant and so cold. Then I realized that although Linda could be cold sometimes, what she never did was go to sleep without her arms around me. Now she was lying, her back to me, facing the wall.

Suddenly a terrible awareness came shrieking into my brain. *She's had an affair! She slept with someone while I was gone!*

I turned toward Linda's sleeping body. I shook her lightly and said, "Linda, wake up."

"What?" she said angrily.

"I have to ask you something — now," I responded. "Linda, did you sleep with someone while I was gone?"

"No," she said simply.

"Are you sure?" I asked, as if she wouldn't know.

"Of course, I'm sure," she said abruptly. "I didn't sleep with anyone. Let me go back to sleep."

I sat up in the bed. I knew she was lying. I don't know how I knew, I just did.

I lay there a few minutes trying to collect my thoughts. Linda got up and headed toward the bathroom. I watched her walk out of the room, then I jumped up and followed her. When she got to the bathroom, she turned and looked at me, square in the face.

"You slept with Rosa, didn't you," I said quietly and firmly.

Linda looked down quickly and said, "Okay, yes I did. And furthermore, I enjoyed it," she said, now looking at me squarely again with anger in her eyes.

For a moment I was speechless. *Loyal Linda?* I thought. How did I know? The anger was welling up inside me. "How could you do that?" I said finally.

"How could I do that?" she started. "You have a lot of nerve. I know you've been having affairs. You think I'm stupid?"

I was confused. I had trusted her completely. I never thought for a moment that I needed to watch her comings and goings. It didn't matter what I had done. It was different when the shoe was on the other foot.

While my mind was whirling, Linda poked in the final jab. "I think I'm in love with her," she said, beginning to cry.

"What!" I screamed. "Oh, that's just great. I hope you don't think you're going to see her anymore?" I asked her with a look of questioning fury.

"I don't know," Linda wailed, now crying profusely.

I looked at her and realized that she really didn't know what to do. For me there was never any question. I didn't fall in love with the women I slept with.

Then the full realization hit me that I might lose her completely over this Rosa. I screamed again, "You can't be serious! That woman is a nut case. You can't ruin our relationship over her. We might have our problems, but that's going from limbo to hell, for sure."

Fear struck me down. My rage was ineffectively covering my deep inner foreboding. Was I actually going to lose Linda?

"Gwen," Linda said after calming down a bit. "I'm going to see her again. I have to find out what I'm feeling. And she's not nuts. She's a very wonderful person."

I knew then she must be in love not to be able to see Rosa's blatant failings. I knew Rosa from Sarah's group originally.

She had left Sarah's and gone to Linda's group, supposedly to help Linda. She was a troublemaker. I had warned Linda about her from the beginning.

I didn't know what to do. I dragged my heavy body into the living room and fell, in shock, into our large blue stuffed chair. I watched Linda slink back to bed. I stayed in that chair all night, the wind totally knocked out of me. I kept thinking, *What am I going to do? I can't lose her now.*

ès 30

A n important realization came upon me as I sat in that chair that night. The truth was that I was just as much to blame as Linda for what was happening to us. Maybe more. It wasn't just the screwing around with other women that had caused this terminal split between us, but the way I had treated her. I drank too much and abused her verbally. I neglected her needs, pushing her aside when she approached me for emotional support. I allowed my anger and resentment about the group to color all of our time together.

I was filled with feelings of guilt, remorse, anger, and shock. I was shaken to my core — not that I accepted the blame completely. But the trust I'd once had in Linda was destroyed. Yes, Linda too was capable of doing the things other people did. She came flying off the pedestal I had put her on.

And Linda could have been more assertive about her needs. She could have let me know more clearly how serious things were for her.

Rosa was just plain bad news as far as I was concerned. She wanted Linda and didn't care that she was being the instrument of our relationship's demise. As a matter of fact, I wasn't convinced that the destruction that was occurring at her hand wasn't a primary motivation for her. At the same time, though, I also didn't doubt for a minute that she probably also was deeply in love with Linda. She, too, was undoubtedly experiencing a lot of pain in this.

So I guess we were all to blame. It was my part in it that I found most painful to accept. I knew I had to take a lot of the responsibility. The big question was, Was it too late to turn things around?

Over the days and weeks to follow, I lived a tortured existence. I should say, *we* lived a tortured existence, because Linda was totally confused and unable to decide what to do. She began staying out a lot, coming home late at night. I always knew that she had been with Rosa. I was thankful that she at least came home. But try as I might, I couldn't keep myself from asking her that question, "Were you with her?"

Linda became furious when I questioned her. She would yell back that it was none of my business where she was. Finally I would get my answer. Almost with pleasure Linda would give in and say yes.

Why did I want to hear the answer? Some sadistic drive in me wanted to know everything. We often stayed up late into the night, arguing. I would try to plead my case so that Linda would stay with me. I admitted my own responsibility and promised Linda I would change.

Linda continued on the edge, repeating that she didn't know what she was going to do. And furthermore she didn't know if she could trust me to change.

She hardly had a kind word for me at all anymore. When we were together she was cold and distant. It was clear that she had held in a lot of anger for a long time.

In between bouts with Linda, I tried to go to work. But I was unable to take care of anyone else. I slept little these days, getting to sleep only after drinking a lot of booze. I had permanent hangovers. I stopped eating. I could think of nothing else but my plight.

After a few weeks I started to look like a ghost. I was thin as a rail, with deep dark circles under my eyes. Other people began to notice. When they asked about me I could think of no alternative but to answer honestly, saying my relationship was in crisis. To my closest friends, I relayed the whole story, seeking and needing their support.

Deadeye, Bam, and Sarah were my main supporters. They listened patiently as I went on for hours about my fears and woes. Somehow analyzing every aspect of the situation seemed to help, a little. My friends were kind and let me obsess. They tried to drag me out to social events and I would go, but just to be with them. I was unable to concentrate on anything other than my fear of losing Linda.

It was during this time that I experienced fear like I had never known. It filled me like a raw unrelenting presence. The only thing that helped was drinking. I had to drink more and more just to dull this monstrous, immobilizing, all-encompassing fear.

I called in sick to work a lot to nurse my hangovers and to drink more. I knew this was not helping Linda choose me, but the torture of waiting for her decision was too much to bear.

After about a month of this horrible existence, Linda approached me one day. "Gwen, I've decided to move out for a while. I'm going to stay at John's. He's invited me to stay at his house until I can straighten all this out for myself."

I flipped out. As much as our lives together now had been miserable, I thought that if she left me, she wouldn't be back. How could I influence her to stay with me if she was gone? Besides, John was Rosa's best friend. I had a pretty good idea that she would be staying there too.

I used all my persuasive ability to try to change Linda's mind. But she was adamant. She said she couldn't think straight with me harassing her all the time. *And I suppose you'll be able to think straight while you're in her arms at John's*, I thought angrily.

She said nothing more but quickly began packing a few things. I sat watching her. As she grabbed her things and worked at packing, she acted as though I weren't even there. When she walked out the door she said nonchalantly, "I may have to come back to get more things later."

Bam! The door closed behind her. I heard her footsteps going down the stairs. Then the bottom door opened and closed.

She's gone, I thought. *She's left me.*

ᚼ31

I kept struggling to get to my job each day. I knew I wasn't much good there, but my survival depended on it. I managed to go most days. All day I would continue to ruminate about what I was afraid was going to happen. Was this the total end of our relationship?

I clung to just a slight hope that Linda would realize the good things we had in our relationship and choose us. I hoped she would be able to see that in any relationship, some things would have to be worked out. And that she would open her eyes to this thing she was having with Rosa — to see just what a relationship with her would ultimately be like. If she thought I was trouble, wait until the glow wore off that one.

Luckily, at work there were a few people I could talk to, because it was impossible for me to hide my suffering. It was a relief to be able to talk to someone about things as they really were instead of having to make up some story.

Martha was a good friend. We had been close since she came to work on my unit shortly after I had started. She was a nursing assistant, and we often worked together on the same team.

Martha had the most beautiful skin color I had ever seen. She was a deep copper brown. Her hair was a soft bunch of salt-and-pepper curls. She had a strong body with arm muscles like I had never seen on a woman. I assumed that the muscles came from all those years of lifting patients.

Since we had first met I had been attracted to Martha. A few months into our friendship I had even approached her about having a sexual liaison. Martha turned me down flat: "I'm not that way," she announced. But she was kind about it and reassured me that if she were "that way," she would definitely go for me.

Our friendship grew even more after that. She was one person at work with whom I could be completely open. Now, that relationship was invaluable. She became my sounding board as I unloaded my woes day after day. I could tell by the way she dealt with me that she was sincerely concerned. Her facial expression when she was with me these days mirrored the way I looked and the trouble I was in. She tried to hold me up with her words of support.

One day, during a discussion, Martha started to express anger toward Linda. She said, "Gwen, it seems to me that woman is taking you for a ride. I think she's playing games. I don't understand all this 'I-can't-make-up-my-mind' business. I think you need to take some action — put her in her place a little. You ain't some kind of rag she can be washing the floor with, you know."

"What do you propose I do?" I asked weakly.

She studied me for a short while, with that pained look still on her face. Then she said, "You remember when you asked me to go to bed with you way back?"

"Of course," I said, looking off into space, a little embarrassed about the incident.

"Well," she said slowly, "how about now? You still feel that way?"

I looked at her directly, now perplexed by her question. "Martha, I don't know what I feel anymore — except scared," I answered. A moment later, I confessed, "If you're asking am I still attracted to you, yes, I guess I am. You're a beautiful woman and I've always been attracted to you."

"Well then," she said with conviction, "I think you and me should do it — show that Linda a thing or two. You can play this game too."

"But Martha, you know I've had lots of affairs," I interrupted.

"Yeah," she said slowly and firmly, "but not with me! I think I could take your mind off your troubles for a while."

I sat thinking, *Maybe Martha's right. Maybe I should focus some energy on a new person instead of pouring myself out on this seemingly lost cause of Linda. Maybe an affair with Martha would help to begin a healing process within myself.*

I looked up at Martha and halfheartedly agreed. "Okay," I said, "when do you want to get together?"

"Come home with me tonight after work."

"It's a date," I said, with a lot more conviction than I was feeling.

After work I followed Martha home to her little apartment in the Bronx. On the way I stopped at a liquor store and bought a fifth of vodka.

"What you need all that for?" Martha asked as I paid for the booze.

"Oh, courage I guess," I said.

"Seems like an awful lot of courage," she said, looking at me with a critical side-glance.

Yeah, yeah, don't bug me now, I thought to myself.

When we got to Martha's place I immediately poured myself a large glass of booze, straight on ice. "Want some?" I offered Martha, raising the bottle toward her.

"You know I don't drink that shit!" she snapped.

"Oh, yeah," I said feebly. "Well, cheers." I lifted the glass and took a good slug. As I sat there drinking, Martha was changing her clothes and picking up the apartment a little. I half watched her. I didn't feel yet in the mood to make love. I hadn't felt that way in a long time. I hoped the alcohol would help to muster up those feelings.

After a while I got that familiar feeling of stress lifting. I began to think about Martha's body and about my feelings for her. I was beginning to get turned on. *I guess there's still some life in me after all,* I thought.

Martha finally sat down next to me on the couch and put her arm loosely around me, resting it on the top of the cushion. She began to play with my hair softly, as she frequently did at work. It was her familiar act of affection. I began to flush. But for some reason my body felt heavy. I didn't think I was able to start this thing, and hoped she would be able to take the initiative.

She was. After playing with my hair for a while, she said, "Well, we gonna do this thing, or what?"

"Yes, I'd like to," I responded weakly.

"Well, come on then." She jumped up off the couch, then grabbed my hand, pulled me up, and led me into her bedroom.

I stood by her bed, slowly starting to remove my clothes. As I did so, Martha quickly stripped herself and lay down on the bed on her back. I paused from undressing for a moment, taking in Martha's beautiful firm brown body. Her breasts were small and perfectly formed, with one slightly larger than the other. Strong muscles bulged from her legs and arms. Her crotch had a scant crop of black curly hair.

Watching me watch her, Martha suddenly threw her arms out to her sides, spread her legs, and said, "Come on, Gwen, come and do whatever you people do!"

With that, I sat down on the bed with a thump, my heavy body needing rest, and began to laugh heartily. It was the first time I had laughed in a long time.

Martha snapped, "What you laughing at?"

"Not you," I spluttered, trying to assure her. "Not you, really." I began laughing again, thinking about how in one fell swoop she had managed to take any of the magic in the situation right out of it. She sat up rigidly, staring at me in anger, waiting for an explanation.

"Martha," I said, finally regaining control, "you don't really want to do this."

"If I didn't want to do it I wouldn't have asked you," she said firmly.

"Look," I said slowly, "I know you want to help me. And I know you care for me a great deal. And I know you want to help me get back at Linda. But unless you really want to make love just for the sake of making love with me, none of that matters. You see what I mean?" I asked, scanning her face questioningly.

"Yeah, I guess so," Martha said, her face now looking a little puzzled. "But I thought that this was what you wanted."

"I did," I explained. "But I wanted it to be a two-way street. I don't want you to make love with me because you feel sorry for me. Even though I really appreciate what you're trying to do. And believe me, I feel very loved by you right now."

Martha nodded, her face relaxed now. She seemed to understand.

We went back to the living room, now fully clothed. I had another drink and we talked a while. Martha played with my hair.

32

When I left Martha's apartment that night for the long trek home from the Bronx to Brooklyn, I was aware of an increased heaviness in my body. Every movement seemed to require a tremendous effort. I just wanted to get home so I wouldn't have to move for a while.

The pain in my psyche was a little diminished by the liquor. I had drunk enough, before I left Martha's, to have a substantial buzz to get me home.

Arriving home, I mustered up the final great effort to walk up the two flights of stairs, throw off my jacket, and pour myself another drink. Then I heaved myself down on the couch, drank, and stared into space.

I was aware even through my tipsy consciousness that something was different. It seemed that the last bit of fight I had had in me was now gone. All hope was abandoned and, with it, all effort to survive.

I knew now that I wasn't going to be able to go to work. I didn't know for how long. But I told myself that maybe after a week or so, I would regain some energy.

That night I drank myself into a coma. Waking the next day, I found myself slumped over on the couch. My pants were wet and there was a large spot in the couch cushion. *Oh,*

God, I thought, *I wet my pants!* As I changed clothes, I was aware that every item of clothing I removed seemed to take a lot of time. I was moving slowly. It seemed as though the whole world had slowed down and was carrying me in its creeping pace. I poured a drink, hoping to blot out any bit of consciousness that might think it had a chance of emerging.

I called work and talked to my supervisor. I told her I was very depressed and needed to take some vacation time, now — that I just wasn't able to make it. Since she had known something about what was happening, she didn't seem surprised. She tried to encourage me to come to work, saying it wasn't good for me to do nothing. But I insisted that I wasn't able to move. Finally, persuaded, she agreed to give me a week, providing I called her every day.

I agreed to call but knew I wouldn't. I felt lucky as I hung up the phone to have a supervisor whom I could be at least partially honest with, and who seemed to be genuinely concerned. I was not yet at the point where the concern and compassion of others didn't help a little.

With that taken care of, I made an inventory of my liquor. I had to go out and get more. I'd get enough to last a while, I thought, so I wouldn't have to go out again.

My pace quickened a little as I completed my task of obtaining a more than adequate amount of booze to sustain me. I was anxious to get all tasks over with so that I could fully retreat into oblivion.

For the rest of the day and night I drank, fell asleep for a couple of hours, woke up, and drank some more. On and on into the next day I continued to blot out my existence.

Periodically when I woke up, I didn't know where I was exactly in the day-night continuum. But it didn't really matter.

During waking periods I thought about Linda. I wondered how she was, what she was thinking. I hoped she wouldn't come to the apartment for any reason. I knew I didn't want anyone to see me like this — particularly her.

Just after waking up from one of my sleeping periods, I heard the doorbell ring. I looked around to determine what part of the day I was in. It looked like early evening. I decided not to answer the door. I had long since unplugged the phone.

But the bell kept ringing and ringing, and the noise of it cleared my mind a little. Resigned, I splashed some water on my face and tried to fix my hair a little. I walked, slowly, feeling very dizzy and weak, down the stairs, and opened the door. It was Sarah.

"Gwen!" Sarah said, with shock and seriousness in her voice. "I've been trying to reach you."

"Oh, yeah?" I said through the blur. "I've unplugged the phone."

"Well, can I come up?" she asked softly.

"Sure, come," I said, motioning her in. "The place is a mess though," I added.

Sarah went into the living room as I put on the pot to make some tea. I went in and sat down next to her. I watched her scan the room briefly. Then her eyes rested on me.

"Looks like you're having a pretty rough time," she noted.

"Yeah, pretty rough," I said with a sigh. We sat in silence for a while. Then I felt obligated to talk.

"I don't know what to tell you, Sarah, that you don't already know. It will just take time to get over this thing, I guess. I just felt like I needed to be alone for a while. I don't seem to have the energy to do anything."

Sarah nodded and said nothing for a few more minutes. Then she sat up straight and started talking. "Gwen, this has been a really hard time for you, I know. I've been through this myself and I know how bad the pain of losing someone can be. I can't really make that easier for you.

"You're right," she continued, "it's something that time will take care of. But what I have to say is about more than your loss." As she said this, she shifted her position a little, and then paused.

"What?" I said, getting a little impatient with her.

"Gwen, I think you have a pretty serious drinking problem," she blurted out finally with a firmness and a smattering of compassion in her voice. She went on, "I think you're an alcoholic." She sat watching my reaction for a moment. There was none. Then she continued, "You've told me about how drinking has caused problems between you and Linda. And I've seen you drink. I just feel that I wouldn't really be your friend if I didn't try to help."

I sat there, numb and helpless. I couldn't fight what she was saying. In a way I knew she was right. In a way I had known this myself. But the thought of having to live without booze sent a shot of fear blazing through me. That fear was the clearest feeling I had had in days.

Sarah was waiting for a response. After a moment, I gathered some strength and said, "Sarah, I don't know, you're probably right. But right now I've got to tell you, I can't even bear the thought of facing one day without a drink. I don't think I could do it, and I'm not sure I want to."

"Of course you can't do it alone," Sarah said, with some impatience. "No one would expect that. But there is a way. How about going to an A.A. meeting with me?" She spoke tentatively now, as if she was afraid I would get angry at her.

I didn't have it in me to get angry. She didn't know how much of the fight was gone in me. But I didn't buy this A.A. thing. How could a group take away the desire to drink? How could a group offer me the same comfort that booze could, the same comforting protection from this fear that was so powerful? No, I just couldn't see it.

I felt the need to persuade her. "Sarah, I'm not ready for anything like that. Once this thing with Linda gets resolved, I think I'll be able to pull myself together. I'm not sure of anything anymore. But I think I'll be all right." I felt the lies slip out so easily.

Sarah said no more. We sat silently. I was wishing she would go so I could have a drink. I no longer felt safe drinking around her.

After what seemed like ages Sarah finally got up to leave. I walked her to the door. I was watching her walk down the stairs when she stopped suddenly. She turned her head a little and just said, "Well, if you change your mind, you know where to find me. You can call me anytime — day or night, okay?"

"Okay," I answered.

After she left I immediately poured myself a large drink and drank it fast. Soon her words and even her presence seemed like a dream. After a couple more drinks the memory of her was almost completely wiped out. But a little bit of what she had said lingered in my mind.

❧33

For several more days I continued my binge. Twice I went out for more booze. Sometimes I would wake up and see an empty bottle and think someone else had been in the apartment, and had drunk the liquor. At one point I even thought Sarah must have drunk some while she was in the apartment. Or maybe someone else came in while I was asleep.

By this time I was feeling quite sick. I began vomiting. It was hard to keep the booze down. I had constant diarrhea. My lips were all dried up. I avoided looking in the mirror, because I wasn't sure whom I was seeing. The person looked something like me. More time went by — semiconscious time.

Then there was a clear remembrance of being in the bathroom vomiting. When I woke up sometime later I was on the kitchen floor. I sat up slowly, but immediately became nauseated and light-headed. I had to lie down again, quickly, so I wouldn't pass out. After a few minutes I tried to get up again.

This time I was able to get myself to the bed, and as I lay there a sudden picture of Sarah popped into my mind. Had she really been here? Yes, I thought so. She had said something about A.A. I looked at my arms and hands as I lay there in the bed. They were dry and very thin. My hands looked like an old woman's hands. *It's that person in the mirror,* I thought.

Oh God, I thought suddenly. *That person is me. I'm killing myself. I'm going to die. I can't even drink anymore. I'll just pass out again and maybe I won't wake up this time.* I had heard stories of people choking to death on their own vomit.

Help! I needed help. I tried sitting up on the bed. After a few attempts, I was able to sit up. Then I stood. Holding onto furniture I walked with shaky legs over to the phone. I dialed Deadeye's number. The receiver shook in my hand. I could hardly hold it to my ear.

She answered groggily. "Huh, who is it?"

"It's Gwen," I answered.

"Gwen, it's three in the morning. What's going on?" Deadeye asked, now awake and with a sound of alarm in her voice.

"Deadeye," I said now in tears, "I need help. I think I'm killing myself."

"I'll be right over," she said without hesitation, then she hung up. The drone of the dial tone lingered in my ear.

I managed to get to the bathroom. I washed my face, brushed my teeth, and drank just a little water. I felt wretched. Periodically my body threatened to buckle from under me, my mind to lose consciousness. But I managed to keep from falling out. I went to the kitchen and sat in a chair by the door, waiting.

I could still hear Deadeye's voice in my ear when the doorbell rang. It seemed like only moments ago that I had spoken to her on the phone. I maneuvered the stairs and opened the front door. Deadeye and Bam were there in the early light of dawn, shopping bags in their arms. Their faces told me that I was right. I had been moving in the direction of my demise.

They helped me back upstairs and poured me some ginger ale. "Take just very small sips, slowly," Deadeye instructed. I saw Bam looking around the apartment. Awe at what I had done to myself overshadowed any embarrassment I might have felt.

As the early morning hours passed, Bam and Deadeye continued to tend to me. They fed me fluids, a small amount of food, and helped me into a hot tub. They washed my hair. They helped me to dress.

The tasks were completed methodically with very little talk. My mind began to clear. My body regained a little of its strength. The healing process began slowly under the loving care of my friends.

Our grooming tasks completed, I sat in a chair with a slight glow of health edging its way through my skin. I had been snatched from death, and my friends had placed me on a new track.

Deadeye sat down next to me, her sleeves still rolled up. Bam was busily picking up the apartment. After a moment Deadeye said, "Gwen, I'd like you to come stay with me for a few days. I don't think it's good for you to be alone right now." Feeling comfortable in the capable hands of these two angels of mercy, I quickly agreed.

Deadeye voiced the arrangements: "Bam will stay too. You can come and go as you want, of course. I'll give you a set of keys."

"Sounds good, D," I said.

Nothing was said about my drinking or whether it would be allowed at Deadeye's. But my body was still bruised enough to recoil at the thought of drinking any alcohol.

Bam helped me pack a few things and we all took a cab to Deadeye's apartment in Manhattan.

❧34

eadeye had a nice apartment with New Mexican and Indian decor, somewhat similar to the condo. It was in a high-rise near midtown. She made up a bed for me in the living room.

I sat in my new space while Deadeye and Bam got ready for work. I felt an incredible peace in this place of Deadeye's. There was a soothing warmth about her home as there was about her.

Bam made some light chatter as they continued to get ready for work. She threw a few light comments and smiles toward me as if to say, Welcome back to the land of the living. I was sure as they walked out the door for work that morning that they had no idea how much they had done for me. A shift had occurred in me that would change my life. I didn't know all of it, right at that moment, but I knew something had changed.

Shortly after they left, I went over to the phone and stared at it for a few moments. Then I dialed Sarah's number. A bright "hello" came after a few rings. I cleared my throat and said, "Sarah?"

"Yes, who's this? Gwen?" she asked, suddenly recognizing my voice.

"Yeah, it's me."

"Oh, hi," she said.

I thought I heard relief in her voice. "Sarah, I think I'm ready for that A.A. meeting now," I spit out.

"Oh, good," she said with enthusiasm. "When do you want to go?" she continued.

"I don't know," I replied weakly.

"Well, there's a noon meeting at a place right near my apartment. How about that one?" she said, thinking as she spoke.

"That sounds fine." I was still weak and only half-resigned.

"Good." Her voice was emphatic. "Meet me at my place at 11:30. We'll have coffee first. Okay?"

"See you then," I responded, still unable to shake my abiding somberness.

I met Sarah that day and attended my first A.A. meeting. I was still weak and not totally clear-headed, but it felt good to be doing something again. When they asked about new-comers, I didn't quite know what to do. Finally, after several other people introduced themselves, I meekly raised my hand and said those words you can never take back: "Hi, my name is Gwen, and I'm an alcoholic." Sarah beamed as she clapped her hands along with the others, congratulating me for saying those words.

Sarah said later that I had a lot of courage. I didn't feel courageous. I felt more like a failure. But what the heck, I was alive.

I left Sarah and went back to Deadeye's for lunch. I could only eat a little toast and drink some tea. My body was still recovering from all the abuse. I thought about what people had said at the meeting. As much as I didn't really feel like drinking at the moment, I still didn't know how these meetings were going to help me. Could I really stop?

For several hours I mulled over the events of the last week — the parts I could remember. And I thought again about Linda. I wondered if I should hope for anything there. She was probably happily rid of me in the arms of another woman.

A thought came into my mind as I sat in Deadeye's place of peace. Maybe I could pray. Maybe God would help me. They talked about God at the meeting. If miracles could happen like those people seemed to think, I could certainly use one.

I decided to go to the Cathedral of St. John's. I had always liked it there when we had gone for concerts. If I was going to talk to God, that seemed like a good place to do it.

≈35

I was winded by the time I reached the top of the stairs of the great cathedral. I was still quite weak, both in body and spirit. As I went through the doors into the church, darkness flooded over me. I walked toward the middle aisle facing the altar. As my eyes adjusted to the darkness, the great beauty and magnificence of the place struck me.

I walked down the aisle, then stopped to look at the incredible stained-glass windows around me. The sun shining through them radiated the many different deep colors that made the images.

It was quiet. Only small groups of people walked in the sanctuary. They stopped at small displays along the sides of the great room, murmuring admiration. I felt a presence. The presence of something other-earthly.

I sat down in a pew and slid in a little. I let the spirit of the place soak into me and quiet my own spirit. I took some deep breaths, slowly, to relax myself. *Well, here goes,* I thought, as I bowed my head to pray.

I prayed for a long time. I presented to God all that was on my mind. Mostly I asked God to take over my drinking problem, to take it on Herself. Then I asked God to help me with Linda. I said I knew I had been partly responsible for losing her and asked for another chance.

For a long time I prayed, sometimes just allowing whatever came to mind to come out in words. Eventually I lost the sense of being in a concrete space and felt instead as though I was floating in a dark hole.

When my mind ˜quieted and my words and pleas stopped, I felt as if I were being enveloped by a soft film. A lightness came over me. A knowledge came to me, simple and fresh. It was the knowledge that all would be taken care of — I had nothing to be afraid of. The anxiety and torturous fear I had been living with was lifted away. I felt in its place a sense of love. Not a love like I had known before. But an all-encompassing love that spread from me like a light, touching all that was within the universe.

When I opened my eyes, I felt a deep sense of elation and serenity. I knew I wasn't going to need to drink anymore. What had seemed impossible an hour ago was now possible. The need for alcohol had left me.

But one question remained. What about Linda? Then, as if a voice were speaking in my head, I heard these words: *She's as afraid as you are. Tell her how much you care.* That sounded so simple. *Could it be that simple?* I wondered.

Still elated and carrying with me the grace of God, I stood up and began walking out of the cathedral. I glided over the stone floor like a ghost. The stained-glass windows and all the other decorations of the great hall seemed to melt away as I passed by.

I swooped down the steps and into the street, continuing in a sort of trance until I came upon a pay phone. I stood and looked at it for a couple of minutes. Then I calmly reached up and dialed Linda's work number.

Linda answered. Her voice betrayed nothing. I said, "Linda, hi, it's me, Gwen."

"Hi," she said, with a hint of some emotion. "I've been thinking about calling you," she continued. "I think we need to talk."

"Yes," I said, "I know. Can we meet at Sanctity's tonight for dinner?"

"Yeah, that would be a good place. Let's meet about seven," she said, her voice now flat and controlled.

"Right," I agreed. "And, Linda," I said quickly, to catch her before she hung up, "Linda, I love you very much."

She said nothing for a moment, then ended the conversation: "I'll see you at seven."

I stood at the phone, hanging up the receiver slowly, unwilling to let go of her. Some anxiety began creeping its way back into me. I couldn't read her at all. I warned myself: I'd better not get my hopes up.

❧36

I arrived at Sanctity's early to settle myself down a little before Linda came. I remembered as I sat there that this had been the first place in Brooklyn where Linda and I had eaten since moving here. I couldn't help but wonder if we had come full circle. Was it also going to be the last?

The place was quiet — moderately void of people — and lent itself to serious discussion. My stomach felt queasy. Even if I had been in totally good health, at that moment, I still doubt that I would have had any appetite.

I wanted so badly to see Linda again. It felt like it had been a long time. My missing her was still a constant gnawing sensation inside me. I hoped with everything in me that this would not be the last time I would be with her, but the beginning of many more times. At the same time, I was afraid to hope. There hadn't been any indication that she would want to get back together. What gave me some strength were those words that I had heard in my ear at St. John's. Maybe God would intervene. I bowed my head for a moment for one last prayer, asking God to soften Linda's heart and give me the right words.

As I raised my head after praying, I saw Linda come through the door, wearing that old familiar trench coat. She looked tired, I noted, as I watched her search the restaurant for me.

I waved. She looked my way, smiled slightly, and came over. "It's getting cold," she murmured as she took her coat off and sat down in the booth facing me. I noticed immediately in her face that life had not been easy for her lately either. Her eyes had aged a little. Her face was drawn. Her usual pink cheeks were pale. A thought flashed through my mind: *She doesn't look like she's in love.*

"It's really good to see you," I said, making direct eye contact. "I've missed you a lot." She looked down immediately. She started to say something but out of anxiety I interrupted her. "How's it been staying at John's?"

"Oh, fine, I guess," she told me. "He's been really good to me. He's tried to make me feel as comfortable as possible."

As she talked, I thought I saw her eyes tearing. *Oh, oh,* I interpreted. *She's having a hard time breaking up with me.*

"I've been staying at Deadeye's for the last couple of days," I told her. "I wasn't doing too well by myself."

"Oh, that's great of her to help," Linda said with a breathy sigh.

"Yeah," I continued, "she and Bam have been terrific. I wish you could get to know them better."

The waitress came over and we ordered our food. After she left, we sat in awkward silence. I thought, *If she's going to dump me, I wish she'd hurry up and get it over with.* The suspense was killing me.

I burst out saying, "Linda, I wish you could give us another chance. I think we still have a lot going for us. I stopped drinking and I'm going to A.A." Earnestly I looked at her. She looked up at me, tears now dripping slowly down her face. She said nothing for a moment, then finally started talking.

"Gwen, I don't feel so terrific about what I've done. You were right about Rosa. The feelings I had for her left as quickly as they had come. It was just a way of getting back at you, I think. More anger than anything else. I'm not seeing her anymore. I guess I've hurt her pretty badly."

"Well," I said trying to bolster Linda a little, "she had to know it was a risky proposition getting involved with someone who had a lover."

"Anyway," Linda went on, "I've missed you too. A lot. Once the anger started to go away I realized how much I really love you. I'm just afraid we won't be able to make it, being so different. And I feel badly about how much I've hurt you. I heard through the grapevine a little about what you've been going through. Would you ever be able to forgive me?" Tears were welling up in her eyes again.

"Linda, what you did I had coming to me," I said quickly. "The alcohol problem was there a long time ago. I just had to get to what the program calls 'my bottom' before I would do anything about it. Your affair and your leaving me just helped me get there faster, that's all.

"We've both hurt each other deeply in many ways," I continued. "But I still believe we can heal." Realizing as I spoke that Linda hadn't come here to break up with me, I felt a tremendous relief and excitement. I saw her fear about trying again, but I also saw a great desire to be together.

Our food came and we picked at it while continuing our conversation. Linda had dried her eyes but there was still a lot of sadness in her face. I waited for her to speak.

"Do you really think we have a chance?" she asked, in an almost childlike way.

"Yes, I do!" I said emphatically.

"Maybe we should go to a couples' counselor," Linda offered.

"We could," I said, a little frightened by that thought. "I'm willing to do anything it takes. I know what I want now. I want a life with you."

"Me too!" Linda said, now bursting into tears. I went over to her side of the booth and put my arms around her. My own face was now wet with tears. We sat and cried quietly for a while.

Then Linda turned her face toward mine, her tear-stained cheeks flushed and wet. She wiped her eyes with a napkin and said softly, "It's good to be home again."

Also from Alyson Publications

☐ **DOC AND FLUFF,** by Pat Califia, $9.00. The author of the popular *Macho Sluts* has written a futuristic lesbian S/M novel set in a California wracked by class, race, and drug wars. Doc is "an old Yankee peddler" who travels the deteriorating highways on her big bike. When she leaves a wild biker party with Fluff (a cute and kinky young girl) in tow, she doesn't know that Fluff is the property of the bike club's president. *Doc and Fluff* is a sexy adventure story but it also confronts serious issues like sobriety, addiction, and domestic violence.

☐ **THE LEADING EDGE,** edited by Lady Winston, introduction by Pat Califia, $10.00. An erotic anthology of writings by and for lesbians that will stir your desires and thoughts. Stories and poems from some of our best known authors and poets. Jewelle Gomez tells the story of a young black lesbian new to New York and her passionate love for another woman. Ann Allen Shockley gives us an interracial lesbian love story set in the antebellum South. Poets Cheryl Clark and Chocolate Waters provide fresh poems that make us think.

☐ **TRAVELS WITH DIANA HUNTER,** by Regine Sands, $9.00. When 16-year-old Diana Hunter runs away from her hometown of Lubbock, Texas, she begins an unparalleled odyssey of love, lust, and humor that spans almost twenty years. Diana makes the most of her journey on her own — but she is rarely alone. The array of women drawn to Diana's wit and body is only overshadowed by Diana's own versatile capacity for meeting their amorous needs.

☐ **BEHIND THE MASK,** by Kim Larabee, $7.00. Maddie Elverton is a fashionable member of English society in the early nineteenth century — a society which limits her aspirations to the confines of the bedroom and the drawing room. But Maddie leads a double life, a life of high adventure as a highway robber. Maddie's carefully balanced world becomes threatened when she falls in love with Allie Sifton, and must compete for the affection of her beloved with the hot-blooded law officer who pursues them both.

☐ **CHOICES,** by Nancy Toder, $8.00. Lesbian love can bring joy and passion; it can also bring conflicts. In this straightforward, sensitive novel, Nancy Toder conveys the fear and confusion of a woman coming to terms with her sexual and emotional attraction to other women.

☐ **MACHO SLUTS,** by Pat Califia, $10.00. Pat Califia, the prolific lesbian author, has put together a stunning collection of her best erotic short fiction. She explores sexual fantasy and adventure in previously taboo territory — incest, sex with a thirteen-year-old girl, a lesbian's encounter with two cops, a gay man who loves to dominate dominant men, as well as various S/M and "vanilla" scenes.

☐ **LESBIAN LISTS,** by Dell Richards, $9.00. Lesbian holy days is just one of the hundreds of lists of clever and enlightening lesbian trivia compiled by columnist Dell Richards. Fun facts like uppity women who were called lesbians (but probably weren't), banned lesbian books, lesbians who've passed as men, herbal aphrodisiacs, black lesbian entertainers, and switch-hitters are sure to amuse and make *Lesbian Lists* a great gift.

☐ **DANCER DAWKINS AND THE CALIFORNIA KID,** by Willyce Kim, $6.00. Dancer Dawkins views life best from behind a pile of hotcakes. But her lover Jessica Riggins has fallen into the clutches of Fatin Satin Aspin, the insidious leader of Violia Vincente's Venerable Brigade, and something has to be done about it. Meanwhile, Little Willie Guthrie of Bangor, Maine, renames herself The California Kid, stocks up on Rubbles Dubble bubble gum and her father's best Havana cigars, and heads west. When this crew collides in San Francisco, what can be expected? Just about anything...

☐ **A MISTRESS MODERATELY FAIR,** by Katherine Sturtevant, $9.00. Shakespearean England provides the setting for this vivid story of two women — one a playwright, the other an actress — who fall in love. Margaret Featherstone and Amy Dudley romp through a London peopled by nameless thousands and the titled few in a historical romance that is the most entertaining and best researched you'll ever read.

☐ **THE CRYSTAL CURTAIN,** by Sandy Bayer, $8.00. Even as a child, Stephanie Nowland knew her psychic powers set her apart. Now an escaped murderer — a man she helped capture — is seeking revenge. Visions of her death and her lover's death fill his thoughts. Stephanie can see them, too. Will her powers, along with the support of the woman she loves, be enough to save them both?

☐ **THE WANDERGROUND,** by Sally Miller Gearhart, $7.00. These absorbing, imaginative stories tell of a future women's culture, created in harmony with the natural world. The women depicted combine the control of mind and matter with a sensuous adherence to their own realities and history.

☐ **GAYS IN UNIFORM,** edited by Kate Dyer, introduction by Congressman Gerry Studds, $7.00. Why doesn't the Pentagon want you to read this book? When two studies by a research arm of the Pentagon concluded that there was no justification for keeping gay people out of the military, the generals deep-sixed the reports. Those reports are now available, in book form, to the public at large. Find out for yourself what the Pentagon doesn't want you to know about gays in the military.

☐ **THE ALYSON ALMANAC,** by Alyson Publications staff, $9.00. Almanacs have been popular sources of information since "Poor Richard" first put his thoughts on paper and Yankee farmers started forecasting the weather. Here is an almanac for gay and lesbian readers that follows these traditions. You'll find the voting records of members of Congress on gay issues, practical tips on financial planning for same-sex couples, an outline of the five stages of a gay relationship, and much, much more.

☐ **THE LESBIAN S/M SAFETY MANUAL,** edited by Pat Califia, $8.00. This handy guide is an essential item for leather dykes who want to learn how to play safe and stay healthy. Edited by best-selling writer Pat Califia, *The Lesbian S/M Safety Manual* deals with issues such as sexually transmitted diseases, emotional and physical safety, and the importance of communication in S/M relationships. There is more information in this slim volume than you can shake a whip at.

☐ **COMING TO POWER,** edited by SAMOIS, a lesbian/feminist S/M organization, $10.00. A collection of writings and graphics on lesbian sadomasochism, *Coming to Power* helped break the silence surrounding the issue of S/M in the lesbian and feminist movements. This groundbreaking book includes advice and political analysis as well as erotic fiction and poetry.

☐ **TESTIMONIES,** edited by Sarah Holmes, $8.00. In this new collection of coming out stories, twenty-two women of widely varying backgrounds and ages give accounts of their journeys toward self-discovery.

Ask for these titles in your favorite bookstore. Or, to order by mail, use this coupon or a photocopy.

– – – – – – – – – – – – – – – – – – – –

Enclosed is $_____ for the following books. (Add $1.00 postage when ordering just one book. If you order two or more, we'll pay the postage.)

1. _____

2. _____

3. _____

name: _____

address: _____

city: _____ state: _____ zip: _____

ALYSON PUBLICATIONS
Dept. H-66, 40 Plympton St., Boston, MA 02118

After June 30, 1992, please write for current catalog.